Assignment Bletchley

A WW2 Story of Naval Intelligence, Spies and Intrigue

Peter J. Azzole

ISBN:0692851445
ISBN-13: 978-0692851449

DEDICATION

To U.S. Navy cryptologists
who have lost their lives
in the performance of duty.

CONTENTS

ACKNOWLEDGMENTS

My sincere thanks and appreciation go to those who graciously volunteered to review and comment on draft versions of this novel. Their critiques and inputs were invaluable in improving the quality of the story.

First and foremost, kudos go to my wife, Nancy, who never failed to provide honest and critical edits and opinions. Also providing significant, candid and insightful editorial inputs were: Sharon Friedheim, Steven Latimer, Linda Müller and Shirley Wang.

I also want to recognize two additional individuals for their assistance in directing me to important research materials on Bletchley Park: Phil Atkins, Head of Site Works, Bletchley Park Trust and Jack Johnson-Walker, Planning Enquiry Officer, Milton Keynes Council, Buckinghamshire, England.

Photo Credits: front cover image, https://commons.wikimedia.org; back cover image, GoogleEarth.

INTRODUCTION

ASSIGNMENT BLETCHLEY is a WW2 historical novel. The story takes place in early 1942 and is mainly set at the British government facility known as Bletchley Park, located in Milton-Keynes, Buckinghamshire, England, about 50 miles northwest of London. Bletchley Park's unclassified title at that time was the Government Code and Cypher School (GC&CS). The unclassified mission was described generally as the school for training of government communications personnel. Its actual mission was primarily communications intelligence (COMINT) and was classified Most Secret (equivalent to U.S. Top Secret).

Upon the declaration of war with Germany on December 3, 1939, this former manor home and country estate became the key facility for the conduct of British COMINT operations. It played an incredibly critical role in the conduct of the war through the ingenuity and dedication of the analysts and supporting staff assigned there. Their successes in exploiting German and other Axis codes and ciphers provided Allied military strategists and tacticians, as well as political leadership, the silver bullet of highly valuable and insightful intelligence.

This novel is intended to teleport the reader into the life of a communications intelligence analyst. It strives to provide an insight into the technologies and challenges involved in COMINT operations during WW2 and to demonstrate the tremendous value of communications intelligence, as well as the absolute need of secrecy in its successes.

Liberty has been taken with certain facts, events, personalities and activities, but all within the framework of history. Blending factual and fictional information facilitated the setting and the telling of part of the very rich

Bletchley Park story in an exciting and intriguing manner.

Names, biographies, descriptions, personalities and activities of active characters are fictitious and any resemblance to those of actual persons is purely accidental.

PROLOGUE

Lieutenant Commander Anthony "Tony" Romella, U.S. Navy, glanced at his watch; it was 6:20pm. He sat back and took a sip of coffee that had now become cold. The latest Top Secret communications intelligence (COMINT) report from the Combat Intelligence Unit, Pearl Harbor, on Japanese Navy operations for the prior day and projections for the future commandeered his total attention for nearly an hour.

The office was abuzz as usual for any day of the week in November, 1941 in OP-20G, the organization code for the headquarters of the Navy's communications intelligence organization. OP-20G occupied the top floor of the Main Navy Building on Constitution Avenue, Washington, DC. Tony was one of the three dozen assigned to it. All of them held the highest security clearances that existed. Their duties included the production of COMINT and management of the Navy's assets and resources worldwide for the exploitation of foreign navy communications. Tony was a key part of that organization and loved every minute of it.

He sipped slowly from his large ceramic mug, staring across the room at the map of the Pacific, ornamented with large pins with colored tags. The fact that major Japanese fleet units, including six aircraft carriers, had been in radio silence for two weeks and intelligence from all sources failed to provide their locations was disconcerting. More alarming to Tony were the contents of decrypted Japanese Navy messages concerning Operation AI. The operations plan to attack location AI, so far, had not provided a date for its D-day nor the location associated with the digraph AI. The details of it could be overlaid onto several key U.S. locations in the Pacific. Determining the location of AI and the date and time for D-day/H-hour was hotly pursued by the Navy intelligence system. Tony was at a loss for anything more that could be done to accomplish that. Something ominous was in the making and the Japanese were foiling the best intelligence system in the world.

Tony's concentration was broken when he realized that the office had cleared. He glanced at his watch, 6:42pm, he arose quickly and headed to the conference room. The occasion was a pre-Thanksgiving office party and a farewell gathering for Tony's mentor, Captain William "Bill" Taylor. Bill was leaving his OP-20G assignment due to urgent orders transferring him to London as the Naval Attaché.

Decrypted Japanese diplomatic messages from Tokyo to their ambassador in Washington, DC in early December 1941 became progressively more indicative of hostilities being imminent against U.S. forces, somewhere. Finally, Tokyo ordered the Ambassador to destroy classified information and equipment in their Embassy. Still, the location of AI, not to mention a large Japanese aircraft carrier task force, eluded the Navy intelligence system. Tony's analysis of the myriad intelligence sources gave him greater concern each day.

Tony was sleeping soundly when the Japanese showed their hand at 7:48am Hawaiian time, Sunday, December 7th, 1941 at Pearl Harbor. That attack sent chaos and confusion rippling through the fabric of the U.S military, especially the Navy. The Navy's intelligence community was now operating at an accelerated tempo in search of answers and projections.

Tony was caught up in the post-attack whirlwind on several levels. Spending 18-20 hours a day in OP-20G was routine. That is, until he received urgent orders to the U.S. Naval Attaché Office, London, England.

1 INTO THE FORAY

U.S. Embassy
Naval Attaché Office
Grosvenor Square, London, Great Britain
Monday, December 22, 1941

Lieutenant Commander Anthony "Tony" Romella, U.S. Navy and Captain William "Bill" Taylor, U.S. Navy were again exchanging a long and animated handshake, but this time on the other side of the Atlantic Ocean. Bill had been a mentor and very close friend to Tony, professionally and personally, for several years. It was no real surprise when Tony received his orders to London. Tony sank back into the dark brown leather chair alongside the Captain's large ancient-looking mahogany desk. He was still a bit out of sorts from the long droning flight from Washington, DC and the time zone difference.

"I can't tell you how damn good it is to see you Tony," said Bill. "Pearl Harbor sure lit a lot of fires under a lot of asses. There's no time or place here for those who can't think fast on their feet and we have a hell of lot of thinking to do. Hopefully, Hitler won't change his mind and decide to attack Britain before we have had a chance to get on top of things. He's focused on the Russian front now, thank God, and intelligence indicates that the U.K. is not in their plans for the foreseeable future. Totally put aside, or so it appears. At any rate, we have some very interesting challenges here and I needed someone I knew and could trust. Someone who could pick up the ball, run with it and not need babysitting. And so, Tony, here you are," said Bill smiling.

Tony nodded, "Here, but with only a few hours sleep since I left DC. The DC-3 is one noisy airplane. It was VIP configured and comfortable, but I could only cat nap. I did crash hard after I got settled into the VOQ here late last night."

Bill smiled, "They told me that you had arrived. At least you got some sleep, but I expected you to sleep in. Knowing you as I do, it was more a thought than an expectation. How's things up in New England?"

Tony shook his head, "As you might guess Bill, my sister and mother aren't happy about my assignment but they said to give you their best regards," he said with a slight chuckle. "We're still dealing with a few issues regarding my late father's business liquidation and estate. They would rather it was me dealing with the lawyers. Hell, they never understood why I even considered making a choice between a math professorship and the Navy. But, they tolerated my DC assignment nicely because I wasn't that far from home. Getting an assignment in Europe with this war going on, well, it worries them. At any rate, I cast my lot with the Navy without regret, and I love the work we do. I'm happy to be here and I appreciate your confidence. So, Bill, uh, why me? And, what's on my plate"

The Captain crossed his legs, selected a yellow pencil from several standing with their sharpened points up in a white ceramic mug emblazoned on the side with the blue letters USN. Bill pulled a notepad from his desk, leaned back and propped the pad on his thigh. Tony knew from experience that there was a list of items on the pad with a small star in front of each one. As each topic was covered, its star would get circled. Bill's traits had been a great influence, teaching Tony forethought, order, detail and logic beyond what Tony acquired on the road to a PhD in Mathematics. "What we have here Tony is a soup sandwich. Everything is chaotic or nearly so and we are dealing with serious military and political issues constantly. Although your official orders are very general, you are in fact going to function as my communications intelligence liaison officer at Bletchley Park, reporting ultimately to me. This position evolved from an idea that Commander Safford conjured up. The communications intelligence sharing exchange meetings that took place in London, Bletchley Park and Washington in the last year or so were not as positive as we had hoped, in the final analysis. But, Pearl Harbor has changed a lot of thinking in that regard."

Tony nodded, "Commander Safford and I discussed intelligence exchange issues, particularly regarding the info that the German Navy was changing their encryption system effective on the first of February. HUMINT and COMINT both tell us the German Navy has redesigned their existing Enigma system with an additional wheel. That will vastly increase the security of the encrypted information. It will effectively shut down the intel on their navy and critically, their submarine force. There's no telling how long it will take us to figure out how to decrypt that stuff, if at all. It will be a terrible loss of intel. So, Safford had me looking for HUMINT or COMINT that might give us some clues on the system's design. Of course, that led to wondering what the Brits might know but weren't sharing. I wasn't directly involved in any general negotiations on info exchange though. I wondered at the time why the Brits were so reluctant, good grief. We weren't holding anything back, hell we gave them complete info on the Japanese Purple code. We couldn't have been more sincere in our intention to cooperate than that."

"Roger that. It was frustrating," said Bill. "But we had people in DC who were hesitant also about sharing everything, which didn't help matters. I think a few key DC personalities were mostly afraid that the Germans would return their focus on England and overrun it. Right now, the Germans seem oblivious to our successes in reading their encrypted communications, but capturing Bletchley would change that. Early on, when I was fairly new on the staff in OP-20, Larry Safford and I talked at length about intelligence sharing and functional augmentation with the Brits. We figured the best way forward was to try and get someone on permanent exchange duty in their Ministry of Defense, or Operations Center or better yet, Bletchley Park where the first levels of analyses were performed. He pulled a lot of strings to get me over here in this billet so I could help lay the groundwork for that concept. Subsequently, OP-20G, as you know, began intimating that the current British Merchant Marine Cypher might be compromised. Larry felt that the Bletchley could use some assistance from us to help solve the Merchant Cypher question as well as the new Enigma issues as fast as possible. So, Larry started cabling me about accelerating the idea of a liaison or exchange officer at Bletchley Park to get insights into what's going on there. He was especially concerned about the plans for increasing the number of convoys of resources to the Brits. Potentially vulnerable encrypted communications systems relating to convoy info could be disastrous. At the same time, the Admiral was growing more concerned about a smooth integration of U.S. and U.K. intelligence resources and thought some eyes and ears at Bletchley Park would be valuable. It was all coming together. When Larry asked me for my suggestion of who might be good for this assignment, he wasn't happy when I offered your name. He absolutely didn't want to lose you. I told him that as a technically competent Lieutenant Commander, you were senior enough to garner respect but not so senior as to seem as merely an overbearing representative. More importantly, I reminded him that you already were butt deep in the new German submarine Enigma problem and how the success of the Moscow counter-intelligence mission you and I completed was absolutely due to your tactfulness, technical knowledge and sheer ingenuity. At that point he agreed."

Tony smiled, "I had no idea all this was brewing. Commander Safford never mentioned it until the orders were approved. I really did appreciate working for him, he is an incredible mind and visionary."

"Well my friend, here you are in the middle of a typhoon," said Bill. "Let me get straight to it. You will have a collateral but very important task, nicknamed Project Cigar."

Tony listened carefully for several minutes as Bill summarized the mission. When the Captain finished, Tony put his head back, closed his eyes and digested what the Captain had just told him. Five years in the Navy's communications intelligence effort leading up to the Japanese attack on Pearl Harbor prepared Tony for technical challenges and surprises, but the assignment just described by the Captain was not exactly of that realm, not by a long shot. It sounded more like an exciting spy story. Tony's mental sorting of the elements of Project Cigar was slightly distracted by the smell of a fresh coat of moss green paint coming from the iron radiators that were creaking as steam rushed into them. The noises of the radiators reminded him of the one in his childhood bedroom and how the dry heat made his nose bleed and his sinuses hurt. Tony stared at the picture of President Roosevelt on the wall behind Captain Taylor. He scratched an itch in the center of his crew cut black hair as his mind wandered. Bill watched Tony's wide set brown eyes open and focus on fresh cracks in the ivory painted wall plaster, evidence of German bomb impacts during the Blitz. Conscious of the Captain's patient gaze, Tony clasped his hands behind his head, looked directly at Captain Taylor and said, "I only arrived in London a few hours ago, Bill. I don't know any of the British Naval Staff in London, let alone anyone at Bletchley Park." He scooted up to the edge of the chair and continued, "Hell, I haven't even met the people assigned to your staff. I'll definitely need some time to gain confidences, resources, connections and hell, just to figure a way to accomplish all this."

The Captain ran a broad open palm over his balding short gray hair, planted his elbows squarely on his desk, nodded and with a fleeting hint of a smile in his freckled face said, "I realize that. But, pardon the tired old phrase, there's a fucking war going on. We don't have the luxury of time. Frankly every day brings something new for me too. I know you will live up to your reputation and capability Tony. It's your project, your pace, your methodology and I'll support you to the best of my ability. I have known you long enough to know you'll be fine."

"Aye, aye sir, I can't ask for more. I'll give you all I have," said Tony.

Bill paused to stuff tobacco into a large mahogany pipe that had a detailed carving of a dragon's head for a bowl. It was one of many in Bill's collection of ornate pipes displayed on a rotating cherry wood stand. Tony sat back, knowing what would ensue. Bill had a knack for elegant conversation transitions and injecting quiet showmanship into dead air with a unique flair. It was designed to give minds time to sharpen, attitudes to mellow or to heighten the impact of the words to follow. Bill turned around to open a red cedar container on the credenza behind his desk and took out a box of matches. He turned back around, slid open the match box, removed a wooden match and stowed the match box in his middle desk drawer. Tony observed in awe the art being displayed by Bill's actions and at the same time, felt a degree of impatience with it all. Bill scraped the match head across the desk surface rapidly enough to ignite it, allowed the initial torch to calm down and the acrid smoke to rise upward, lit the pipe and puffed on it intermittently. "By the way Tony, sorry I couldn't make it to your promotion party. Getting Evelyn and the kids packed and moved to Ellicott City was just too much to do in too short a period of time. Those Lieutenant Commander stripes look mighty fine on you though."

Tony smiled, mainly with relief that the requisite calming had been accomplished, "Thanks Bill. Your fitness reports played an important role in that and I'm both humbled and grateful. Getting back to Project Cigar sir, what's the cover story?"

Bill nodded, "I put a lot of thought into that. Your original liaison assignment is perfect for that. I made sure the Brits knew of your personal role in the Navy's direction finding network planning, your analysis of German U-boat communications systems and German communication intelligence programs. Bletchley Park's operation is heavy with Cambridge mathematicians so your math PhD, albeit not from Cambridge, will bring you some credibility. Your credentials have been well established with the Ministry of Defense and the Admiralty's Operations Center, for the sake of brevity, the MOD and OpCen, respectively. They are glad the U.S. has entered the fray, at the same time, they are very provincial at Bletchley, even paranoid that Bletchley's critical functions will be discovered. They also don't like the thought of us possibly meddling or running roughshod over their ways and means. To get things moving, I arranged a meeting on Wednesday with key players at the MOD and OpCen. A Bletchley Park representative will be present, although I'm not sure who that will be yet. This will be a good introduction to kick off your work and get the interactions and politics sorted out. Whatever security papers they want you to sign is fine."

"Aye sir."

"Good. Now, back to Cigar. For background, Ambassador Winant received a Top Secret dispatch from the White House directing that this investigation be conducted and completed as soon as possible. The rumor mills and witch hunts have started boiling at high levels in DC on every aspect of the Pearl Harbor attack. One specific rumor in question, if proven false, will allow the President a good measure of peace of mind. But, as you might guess, if it turns out that the allegation of Churchill holding back on critical intel about the Pearl Harbor attack is true and the press or anyone else finds evidence to that effect, Roosevelt will have to rethink his level of trust with Churchill. I've been told that Edward R. Murrow has been stretching his press credentials to snoop around London at many levels. He's apparently trying to get more details about Churchill's frustration with the U.S. reluctance to get into this war sooner. He seems to me to be very interested in the British perspective on a range of subjects, but has now focused on their attitude about intelligence sharing with the U.S. He may have picked up a hint about our frustrations in this area somehow and if so, we probably don't have a lot of time. I shudder to think what impact it would have to Roosevelt's relationship with Churchill if some unflattering tidbits of Winston's thoughts, or even of his staff, leak out in the press, regardless their validity. Or vice versa for that matter."

"But, Cigar seems like a big risk to take, politically," said Tony.

"That's not our decision. The President personally ordered it. He can deal better with knowing the truth beforehand rather than getting surprised, like any of us. At any rate, outside of a few people in the White House and State Department, only the Ambassador, you and I know about Project Cigar. It must stay that way." Bill winked, "I expect you'll find ways to use the access at Bletchley to full and clever advantage." Tony smiled with an acknowledging nod. Bill went on, "Your primary mission, as formally directed by OP-20G, is assisting in any and all ways in exploiting the new German Navy Enigma system and defining Germany's intensified efforts and effectiveness in breaking our joint Merchant Marine and Naval cyphers. Project Cigar lurking in the background, of course. For what it's worth, engineering teams in their MOD and Washington are working on a more robust cryptographic system for use by the North Atlantic convoys to the U.K. I'm sure they are going to be uncomfortable even considering the current cyphers might have been penetrated by the Germans. Hell, so are we for that matter. In any case, don't ruffle feathers and steer clear of controversy. They aren't thrilled with having Yanks in their inner sanctum at Bletchley, so it will not be a simple set of relationships. They have worked hard to keep the communications intelligence aspect of Bletchley Park operations a secret. They are very proud of their ULTRA reporting system for reporting information gleaned from decrypted messages and have fought hard to keep control of it and ensure the distribution of it is extremely limited. They are fearful in general that somehow, one day, the Germans will learn what's really going on at Bletchley and bomb it or God forbid, infiltrate. By the way, the unclassified title and cover story of Bletchley is that it's the Government Code and Cypher School, they use the acronym GC&CS, where classified communications system training is conducted for all service branches and government."

"Understood," said Tony.

"You'll report to Captain Rhys Hardcastle, Royal Navy as soon as you arrive at Bletchley. He's the installation commander. You'll need your best judgement and diplomacy to deal with him. In that line of thought, don't use his first name, I'm told he rarely uses it and considers his first name inappropriate for those junior." Bill spent a few minutes providing a full profile of Hardcastle. "And that, Tony, is everything I know about the dead serious Captain Hardcastle."

"Thank you Bill, it's good to know those things in advance, I'm sure I can navigate the Bletchley seas."

"One last thing, it goes without saying, but I must," said Bill. "You cannot do or say anything that will draw British suspicion to Cigar. You just cannot get caught pursuing this."

Tony knew Bill well enough to catch the body language that indicated this meeting was over. "Understood! I assume you will maintain arm's length?"

"Yes," said Bill rising from his chair, "from this moment on, you're on your own with Cigar. We will be forced to deny any knowledge of your actions in that regard. If you are compromised, we'll have to transfer you back to DC immediately, ostensibly on suspension of duty pending an investigation. Be very discreet. Keep me informed. Find a private cottage you can rent, or buy if you must, if one's even available. We'll reimburse you for the rent or purchase. It would really be best if you were bunking independently."

"Aye, aye, Captain," said Tony as he came to his feet. "I didn't have time to do any Christmas shopping before I left DC. I will probably catch hell from my mom and sister, bless their hearts, but I'll find something interesting for them and get it mailed. Better late than never."

Bill grinned, "Bring the packages to me, I'll get them into the diplomatic mail, it'll be faster." They shook hands.

Tony added, "I have a feeling that the Christmas of 1941 is not one I'll ever forget."

Bill laughed, "By the way Tony, tonight's movie here in the embassy theatre is Honky Tonk, with Lana Turner, at 1900. Isn't she one of your favorites?"

"She is indeed, I'll be here at 1845 sharp."

"Good, and Tony, you should be able to find some fun things to do in Piccadilly Square and the Red Cross has clubs all over London. Lieutenant Ryan Jacob, also single, has been here on staff for a few months, I'm sure he can fill you in on what to see and where to go."

"From what I could see, just from the ride from the airport and stepping out for breakfast, London is awash with uniforms from several countries. I'll have a lot of competition," Tony said smiling.

"More than several, there's something like a dozen or so countries worth of uniforms here. At any rate enjoy yourself. Depart for Bletchley when you feel you're ready. Take some time to meet the staff and some intel people at the Admiralty and the MOD. Ryan Jacob can tell you who you should talk to."

2 A WALK IN THE PARK

Tony spent a few days consulting with the attaché staff and with officers in the British Admiralty, Operations Center (OpCen) and Ministry of Defense (MOD). It was time to move on to GC&CS (Bletchley Park), report to Captain Hardcastle and settle into a work routine that promised a significant challenge to his technical and diplomatic skills.

Tony managed to talk the embassy motor pool out of a jeep. It wasn't that difficult since they had a jeep that was missing its canvas top and a few other items due to being cannibalized, thus it was relatively undesirable, especially in the winter. One could also easily do without a speedometer, right side windshield wiper and rear seats. All in all, this jeep was in no way a valuable resource to anyone. Tony, being relatively wealthy, was more accustomed to fine cars, but being practical was more important at the moment. He controlled his annoyance with the motor pool's red tape, signed several documents acknowledging his responsibilities for the jeep and other details involving the transfer of custody of Army property. Then there was the briefing on pertinent British driving laws and signage prior to being issued a military driver's license. At long last, he was returning salutes from the sentries on the embassy gate as he passed through. He referred to the handwritten route instructions Bill's Yeoman gave him, picked up the A5 and headed north on the remaining 45 mile trip to Milton-Keynes. It was amazing how quickly the route took him out of evidence of Luftwaffe bombing. London had many rubble piles and damaged buildings in the process of being cleaned up. Here and there were skeletons of burned out buildings and storefronts with boards where windows once displayed wares. Those were very depressing sights but there was reconstruction and repair activity everywhere. Much had already been done, much remained. Recovery efforts overrode the general depression of the Londoners and spoke volumes about British morale.

The jeep's rigid suspension sent a jolt from every bump in the road straight through the poorly padded seat to his body. The missing muffler numbed Tony's ears with a loud raucous exhaust that made the jeep sound more like a fire engine. His long underwear, bridge coat, gloves, scarf and hat proved only moderate protection from the icy cold and humid air of this thickly overcast day. The drive was uncomfortable and bone chilling. Tony daydreamed about his silver 1938 Cadillac convertible coupe and hoped his sister was enjoying it. This assignment will have many new experiences and myriad Spartan conditions to offer, he thought, all of which would be good for his character. Yes, that's it, character development, he mused and smiled. Tony 's love for the Navy and his specialty of communications intelligence in particular far outweighed any disadvantages that would be coming his way. He was simply in awe of being part of something so very unique and special. Having Top Secret material in his hand on a routine basis was an opiate for him, a driven man of means, confidence and ego.

The highlight of the noisy, rough ride to Bletchley Park was the respite from the elements and a fish and chips lunch at the Goat's Head Pub midway. The regulars were genuinely friendly despite the fact that he gave them a good run for their money at the dart board. It would have been easy to linger for more than the time it took to eat and enjoy a pint of room temperature half-and-half by the wood fire in that quaint pub.

Just about the time his patience was getting thin with the cold and the jeep, he arrived in Milton Keynes, Buckinghamshire and soon, the right turn onto Wilton Avenue was before him. Shortly thereafter, he was at the Bletchley Park main gate with two brick sentry enclosures either side of the road. It seemed unlikely that Bletchley Park, a former private estate of high luxury but now a very important node in the British defense system, would be located in an area of agriculture, horse farms and industry. But that was the point. Tony presented his documents to the guard that came to his jeep. As directed, he pulled his jeep to the side and waited patiently for calls to be made. Finally, his orders were returned, along with a simple map of the installation and he was waved into Bletchley Park. He parked his jeep at the military vehicle parking area on the right just inside the gate. He traded small talk with the civilian and military mechanics at the garage and got down to the brass tacks of arranging for long term parking, fueling and maintenance of his jeep. Accomplishing that, he carried his sea bag and leather attaché case to the Mansion. The Mansion, as it was nicknamed, was the former manor house of the estate, which no doubt had a long and interesting past. It was now the headquarters building of the GC&CS aka Bletchley Park. The Park had been enlisted into sensitive government service at the outbreak of war with Germany, owing to its remoteness from London and German bombing targets. He lingered a moment as he entered the semicircular driveway in front of the Mansion, musing that it reminded him of a gingerbread house. It had a Tudor-style look, two stories, mainly red brick with concrete corner and window trimming. There were beautifully detailed dormer windows. Several tall peaks and chimneys rose elegantly from the roof as did a few radio antennas. Just to look at it evoked a historic sense and a curiosity of its grand pre-war days. Captain Taylor mentioned that Bletchley was quite a melting pot of British civilian government workers and all branches of British military personnel. He saw evidence of that already in the people that were milling about in serious hurry.

Tony passed between the two six foot gargoyles guarding the marble-arched recessed main entrance and opened one of the two thick hardwood doors. Just inside, on the right, was a marble columned entrance to a lounge lit naturally by an impressive skylight the size of the room. An armed Royal Army corporal, standing behind a small desk, motioned for Tony. He presented his orders and ID to the corporal. Tony's name was found on a list and the corporal returned his documents. Pointing at a floor plan on an easel, the corporal pointed out the short hallway opposite the lounge, off of which was the door to a room labeled 37-Admin. This was the office of Captain Nigel Hardcastle, Royal Navy, the Park's commanding officer. Hardcastle was responsible for logistic support to the Park's mission and was in general command of the military and civilian personnel.

Hardcastle was retired from the Royal Navy and was a deep draft freighter captain when the war broke out. Hardcastle's degree in electrical engineering, his reputation for dogged determination and other political factors, resulted in his recall to active duty to get Bletchley staffed and equipped for wartime operations. Hardcastle wanted, instead, to be a convoy commodore and fought the Admiralty and Ministry of Defense tooth and nail to get that, but it was all in vain.

Captain Taylor's briefing about Bletchley and on Hardcastle in particular, sped quickly through Tony's mind as he made the short walk to Room 37. Tony knocked on the door and entered. On the opposite end of the room was a Royal Navy Petty Officer that looked up from her typing, "Good afternoon sir, may I help?" she asked. The other desk in the room was not occupied. The presence of a bridge coat with captain's shoulder boards and a Royal Navy senior officer's cap on a clothes tree standing off to the side made it obviously the desk of Captain Hardcastle.

"Lieutenant Commander Anthony Romella, U.S. Navy to see Captain Hardcastle," said Tony as he propped his seabag against the wall by the door.

She stood and motioned toward a straight back chair with a modestly padded, leather covered seat and back, alongside Hardcastle's desk, "He is expecting you sir. He will be back shortly, please have a seat."

He expected that the term shortly might not be the case. The yeoman was focused on her work, so he put his brief case alongside his chair and busied his impatient mind with cataloging the room, as an intelligence officer is want to do. He noted how effective the white walls were in preserving window light during dull winter days like this one. Dark oak flooring was in marked contrast with the walls. A high ceiling, sculptured artistically, had but one light which hung high above the Captain's desk. It was clearly furnished and outfitted for practicality, not luxury or status as he was sure it once was. The room was large enough for perhaps three full sized desks, but there were just two, plus a built-in corner desk that had a stack of documents on it. There was a drafting table in the other corner of the room, angled slightly forward, with several large architectural blueprints on it. Many others were rolled and stowed on a shelf under the table. The drawings no doubt related to the large number of construction projects Hardcastle was implementing to provide work space for the rapid and continued influx of workers.

A large part of the outer side of the room had a deep nine pane bowed window structure which was large enough to comfortably nestle the Captain's desk. The structure protruded sufficiently to give the Captain a good corner view of most of the mansion's front driveway. Boxed radiators under the bow windows provided, aside from heat against the drafts, a ledge for keepsakes. Framed 8" x 10" photos of King George VI and Prime Minister Winston Churchill sat on the ledge to the right of his desk. Tony noted that the Captain kept a relatively clear desk, with just a phone, a stack of papers and documents in a basket, a wooden ink pen holder with a glass ink well, a briarwood pipe sitting in a black marble ashtray, a lamp and a large tea cup and saucer. A document the Captain was working on before he left his desk bore the red stamp marking MOST SECRET on its cover.

The yeoman's desk was positioned on an angle in one corner of the room in front of two enclosed right-angled storage cabinets affixed to the two walls. An electric fan, a six-drawer card file, a paper hole punch and other small office equipment items sat on top of the storage cabinets. Her small desk had room only for a typewriter, a phone, a plain tea cup and saucer, a brimming in-basket and classified pages of a document being prepared from scrawling on yellow lined pages.

It wasn't long before Captain Hardcastle hurried through the door, nodded at Tony on his way to his yeoman's desk where he picked up a phone message. He read the message, turned and approached Tony.

"Good afternoon Captain. Lieutenant Commander Tony Romella reporting for duty sir," said Tony as he stood and put his hand forward.

Captain Hardcastle was not at the London meeting in the OpCen Tony attended, so this was their first meeting. "Good afternoon Lieutenant Commander," said the Captain in a strong, gravelly voice as he shook

Tony's hand with a very firm grip, then motioned at Tony's chair. The light of this dingy day fought its way through slightly yellowed lace curtains on the bow windows and provided the only light for the Captain's desk. Heavy black drapes for night blackout were pulled back to the sides. There was an antique ship's lamp on his desk with an amber wick dangling in straw colored oil, but it was not lit. Hardcastle was apparently frugal with the Park's power and resources. "Let's get this sorted Lieutenant Commander," said Hardcastle as they took their seats. The Captain's bluish gray eyes peered out coldly from under bushy gray eyebrows set on a very weathered face. His bulky tall body, square chin, manner and voice all combined to make a formidable character. Tony, in great contrast, was probably close to half Hardcastle's age at 31, subtly handsome and with a smooth deep voice. Tony's relatively dark Italian complexion differed from the Captain's very light skin, but their tall muscular builds were comparable. Hardcastle opened his center desk drawer and removed biographical documents on Tony. "The Admiralty says you have notable COMINT experience, refined manners, high intellect and pleasant comportment. I suppose we'll find that out in due course."

Tony nodded sharply. He was aware that the Captain was sizing him up and prepared himself accordingly.

Hardcastle took a deep breath and gripped one hand firmly with the other in front of him and rested them on his desk, "We didn't ask for help from the Yanks, but Churchill and the MOD seem to think it would be useful. The Admiralty agreed to allow you to work here. Make bloody damn sure you don't stray from your assignment. I have been briefed by MOD on your assigned duties." The Captain pushed an installation map across his desk to Tony that had buildings circled in pencil. "You thus are granted access to these buildings only, the first floor only of this mansion, former garage in the rear of this building, the A Block building and operations huts four and eight, exclusively. You will be briefed in due time on the activities in these buildings as your need to know dictates. Your primary work space will be located in A Block, the Naval Intelligence area. We're bulging at the seams here now, so the old garage has been converted to office space. There is a small desk in the loft out there with a phone that will be made available to you on a shared basis with the traffic analysts up there. Report to that office the first thing each day. You will get your daily briefing materials and messages there before you proceed to A Block for analytical work. My yeoman will assemble those briefing materials and messages at 0600 and put them on that loft desk. She'll show you where that desk is when we're done here. She will also be available to you for limited administrative support."

"Aye, aye sir," said Tony.

"Right. Now then, Second Officer Petra Wilkinson controls the naval intelligence document storage in A Block. She has been instructed to make available those documents you request that appear to be pertinent to your mission. In the event of a question of pertinence, she has been ordered to refer your request to the appropriate senior analyst for a determination. Any and all unsettled disputes will be brought to my attention. We operate with a strictly controlled access here."

Tony nodded, "Aye, aye sir."

"I realize that the MOD obtained your signature on the Secrecy Act and related documents, however, I have my own as well." The Captain then pulled a document from his in-basket and read from it, "You may only carry documents from your work space in A Block to and from this building and Huts four and eight. When not in your use, documents will be stowed only in A Block. You may not copy or otherwise transmit any material or reports, classified or unclassified, to anyone without the express permission of Captain Hardcastle or his successor. You will not discuss classified information with anyone, anywhere, at any time, without an absolute need for you or them to know it. Do you understand your access and security restrictions?"

"Aye, aye sir," said Tony, feeling uncomfortable with the Captain's demeanor.

The Captain pushed the document he just read to the side edge of the desk opposite Tony, dipped a simple military issue pen in an ink well and placed it by the document. Tony scanned the paper and signed on the line above his name at the bottom and pushed the pen and paper back towards Hardcastle.

"Right," the Captain continued, "now, uh, pending the completion of A Block, we still have a large part of the German Navy analytical group on this ground floor and the first floor. Your access is limited to those floors. MI6 officials are on the second floor and you have no need to know what their functions are and have no access to that floor," he paused for Tony's acknowledgement.

"Aye, aye sir," Tony replied.

"Jolly good, now then, I am aware that you have a PhD in Mathematics. Thus you no doubt are aware that Alan Turing, Gordon Welchman and other brilliant mathematicians are working here and that you are probably looking forward to meeting them. You will NOT pursue them and you will not speak to them unless they initiate a conversation. They are incredibly busy with near impossible challenges and I do not want them distracted, is that understood?"

"Aye, aye sir," Tony replied."

"Now Lieutenant Commander," the Captain continued with marked emphasis, "concerning fraternization. I am told you are unmarried and have means independent of your Navy salary. We have a preponderance of ladies here at Bletchley, civilian and military. All miss their pre-war lives, friends, husbands. They have stressful jobs and are vulnerable in many respects. Romantic entanglements will result in interference and degradation of performance, good order and discipline. Therefore, I must ask you not fraternize with them."

Tony was taken back and quickly replied, "Captain, in the U.S., civilians above a certain grade are considered equivalent to officers and socializing among officers is not considered fraternization-"

Hardcastle cut him short, "May I remind you Commander, this is not the United States."

"Understood sir," said Tony, feeling his Italian blood beginning to boil, "I merely want to clarify the ground rules. I'm sure there will be social interactions and functions in which I'll wish to participate and I want no more or less restriction than other male officers under your command."

Hardcastle glared at Tony for a moment, sensed determination equal to his own and realized he was risking embassy and Admiralty ire if he placed undue protocol restrictions on Tony. He pondered a bit then said, "Your point has merit, I shall provide you with civilian equivalencies. Socializing with unmarried female officers and equivalent civilians will not be considered unauthorized fraternization. However, I expect you shall bloody well conduct yourself with utmost honor and discretion."

Tony nodded smartly, "Aye, aye sir."

"Will you be going directly to A Block Lieutenant Commander?" asked the yeoman. "If you like, I'll stow your seabag in the reception lounge and you can pick it up when you are ready to go get sorted for the evening."

The sprawling multi-wing concrete structure with a small sign at the entrance simply identifying it as 'A' was a short walk from the mansion, around an expansive but brown and dormant lawn. Tony admired the landscape as he walked, visualizing the lake in summer as peaceful and beckoning, alive with birds and small animals. For now, it was mostly blanketed by a sheet of ice and devoid of wildlife. The telltale evidence on the ice of heavy use for skating intrigued him, something he hadn't done in many years. Goal frames on the lawn told the story that in fair weather, the men and women stationed on this highly secret base retained their outlook for fun and exercise. He saw several simple a-frame wood-sided huts, apparently hastily built at the start of the war. They seemed to be nestled throughout the estate, where people busily toiled on monumental intelligence challenges. More substantial concrete buildings were being added along the road where A Block was located.

Tony entered the ground floor door of the building's wing notated on the map the Captain gave him. A civilian lady greeted him as he entered,

"Good afternoon sir, this way please. They told us you were on your way. My name is Molly Lawson, Royal Navy civil service."

"Lieutenant Commander Tony Romella, USN ," he replied.

They shook hands briefly, entered a door on the left off the small foyer, "My pleasure sir, this way please," she said and ushered him down a long sparsely lit hallway. It smelled of fresh paint and concrete. They exchanged nods and smiles with people they passed, some civilian, some military. Most of the offices along the way had their doors closed. The two offices that were open had cluttered desks and wall maps but the analysts were temporarily absent. None had nameplates or titles, just room numbers but all were surely in use. There were sounds of construction taking place on the floor above which no doubt perturbed the analysts. The concrete floor in the hall had no covering, but then, none was required. There was no hint of perfume from Molly; but such things were probably a war-time luxury not wasted in working spaces. Her perky manner, freckles, bright dimpled smile and strong Scottish brogue was very charming. Her plain black shoes with wide one inch heels made distinct contact sounds as she walked. Her plain blue tartan wool dress that was hemmed half way to her ankles made its own subtle noises.

"That's a unique sculpted design and blue hue on your sweater Miss Lawson, a shade of my favorite color," he said, as they turned the corner to the left and proceeded down another a short hallway past restrooms on the right leading to another wing.

"Mum knit it for me as a Christmas gift, thank you. I assist Second Officer Wilkinson in the archive section," she explained as they turned to the left and continued down another long hall. "There's just the two of us in there working our bloody fingers to the bone."

Tony chuckled, he couldn't see her face but could hear the smile on it, "May I call you Molly?" she nodded in a sort of non-committal way. He continued, "You may call me Tony if you wish."

"We have our rules Commander," she said. She stopped at a door marked simply 17 and motioned for Tony to enter. Inside the door was a long room painted in very light tan, with an open area large enough for 3 desks, a small table and two file cabinets, all of wood construction. Lights with white and green ceramic coated metal shades hung from the ceiling over their desks. The far end of the room was fully partitioned into a storage area that had a door that was ajar. Outside the storage room there was a woman working at a desk opposite what apparently was Molly's desk. She looked up as they entered.

"Lieutenant Commander Romella, USN please meet Second Officer Petra Wilkinson, WRNS. Second Officer Wilkinson, this is Lieutenant Commander Tony Romella." The woman rose to greet Tony. He figured her to be about his age, tall and trim, with curly brown hair in an up do. Her features were plain but very pleasant and free of makeup.

"My pleasure Second Officer, Wilkinson" said Tony as they shook hands. Molly went into the adjoining room and fetched a wood folding chair and placed it beside Petra's desk for Tony. The storage room was about 10 foot square, with two small tables and several wood folding chairs in the center of the room. Five-foot-tall multi-drawer wooden file cabinets stood side-by-side along the sides and back walls. Some had drawers designed for 3x5 cards, some for 5x7 cards, but most were for letter sized documents.

"Please have a seat Commander," said Petra routinely, "Welcome to our new working area. It's temporary until the central registry in C Block is completed. As you noticed, construction continues here in A and B Blocks. C Block construction just begun. As soon as most of the first floor here in A was completed we began moving some of the German Naval Intelligence functions in from the Mansion and Hut 4, giving the analysts some proper working space. We moved into this room about a month ago and began consolidating storage of certain German and Japanese Navy documents."

Tony nodded, noting her distinctly professional demeanor while hiding his pleasure about potential access to Japanese COMINT, "I noticed the hustle and bustle of construction and concrete work down the road and elsewhere too for that matter. MOD mentioned the juggling act and planning challenges of bringing in more people to increase productivity and providing work space and living quarters for them."

Molly took Tony's hat and put it on the table across from her desk. "This is your work table," said Molly.

"Thank you Miss Lawson, or is it Mrs.?"

"It's Miss, Commander," she said, blushing. "Spot of tea sir?"

"Yes please, just a hint of sugar and milk."

Molly laughed, "How does just a spot of milk suit you?" He laughed and nodded, "Even better, thank you, unless it's sheep or goat!" Molly shook her head in mock disgust and departed.

"Right. Let's talk about the kinds of information you need," said Petra.

Tony sat down, "What I'm looking for are decrypted messages to or from any German high command or shore-based command that are to or from other commands, combatants or merchant ships, that in any way refers to or discusses the German Navy's new design for their Enigma system, including operating instructions. They are calling it TRITON."

"Right. For your information, Hut 8 analysts have nicknamed the German TRITON system as SHARK," she injected.

"OK, noted. Also, I'm interested in anything relating to Allied merchant shipping, shipping lanes, maritime cargo or troop shipments and the like. I'm looking for evidence that they are gleaning intelligence about Allied shipping, including ship-shore communications channels of any kind.

Nothing of intelligence or operational value should be getting transmitted in the clear by the Allies, so anything the German Navy, their B-Dienst intelligence organization in particular, know about those things is either from their success in decrypting cypher systems or operations codes, a spy, loose lips or procedures, or just a lucky guess. In any case, I need to analyze such instances to determine the origin of the information they have."

Petra took advantage of a pause, "Is the London Operations Center no help to you Yanks? I mean…"

Tony interrupted, "The OpCen and MOD have been invaluable, of course. They do share ULTRA level and lesser classified intelligence, but timing is of the essence in some cases, as well as completeness, which is the real crux of the matter. It's expected that filtering decrypted messages for immediate operational value can easily overlook something less evident. Delays in reporting something subtle or which is deemed merely of longer term strategic value could be critical. We're trying to reduce the off chance that something inconspicuous but of high value is not reported or just not reported quickly enough to prevent a loss of merchant shipping to U-boats. Washington felt this was the most effective and least risky way of monitoring this possible threat and minimizing the loss of our merchant ships. The British analyst's general focus is just not the same as mine and for good and just reason. Plus, the U.S. is just as concerned about the impact of the potential intelligence loss when SHARK goes into effect on the first of February. We're prepared to put all necessary resources on this so that between us, we can recover our ability to exploit it as quickly as humanly possible."

She paused briefly to think, then nodded. "Jolly good!"

Molly returned with a cup of tea that had vapor rising into the cool air in the room. "Thank you very much Miss Lawson, even the short walk over from the mansion was chilling. This will go down good!"

"Well, it sounds like a you have your work cut out for you," said Petra, "anything we've decrypted from or related to the German Navy is stored here, including naval subject matter in German High Command communications. Once it's no longer of use to the analysts it's sent to us, so it's not necessarily timely."

"Excellent. That will be just fine," said Tony

"Quite. Uh, does Washington think there's a leak or cypher weakness with merchant communications?" asked Petra.

Tony took a deep breath, "They're just as suspicious and alert as they must be at all times. As you probably know, B-Dienst got into Royal Navy Merchant Cypher Number Two last summer. Since your cryptographic hardware is essentially the same as ours, and use the same cypher settings, it follows that breaking into yours is also breaking into ours for the same key settings."

She nodded, "But no evidence yet on them getting into Cypher Number Three?"

"Not that I know of," he said. It wasn't useful to reveal all he actually knew about suspected vulnerabilities at this point. "But it is probably too soon to tell. We have not looked at enough decrypts or perhaps not the right ones, to gauge the security of the current cypher. It's not practical for Bletchley analysts to send us everything they glean and your MOD realizes that. Washington and MOD agreed that I could get a more complete look here at Bletchley."

A hint of a smile appeared on her face, "Well Lieutenant Commander, you certainly have our support. We sometimes have hundreds of messages a day that might be of interest to you."

"Without a doubt. When can we get started?" he asked.

She nodded, "Capt. Hardcastle told me he briefed you on the rules established for your access." She pulled a sheet from her in-basket and skimmed through it and looked up, "I must emphasize that you must make all requests for documents through this office. You are not authorized to visit the huts or discuss anything with the analytical groups directly unless I arrange it. It's crackers enough in the huts without your unannounced interruption. Also, we call our storage room the vault and I must ask that you not enter it. We'll retrieve anything you need from it. Please pardon my frankness with all this, sir." She paused for him to acknowledge.

"Yes ma'am, I understand," he said fighting off feelings of annoyance. He felt his ears getting red, "I understand the need for restrictions and will certainly abide by the rules."

"Brilliant," she said, "I am glad you aren't offended. And you may call me Petra, formality will be bloody silly in our circumstances."

He laughed, "Well, I damn sure am offended, but we'll make it work. And please call me Tony, Petra."

Her eyes locked with his for a moment, her face expressionless, then she flashed a very brief smile. It was clear she wasn't sure that he was kidding. He was happy to keep it that way. She reached into one of the 20 pigeon holes in an unpainted wooden box that stretched across the front of her desk, "Let me show you what decrypted German Navy messages look like when they arrive here. This one, like all others, has a sheet attached that documents the date, time, how, when and where the message was intercepted, when and who decyphered it, who translated and reviewed it, what, if any action was taken and to whom in Bletchley it was routed. If it was specifically reported upon, a copy of that report is attached also. In this case it was and as you can see, it was sent through the ULTRA channel both to our Operations Center in London and to OP-20G in Washington, DC." She handed it to him.

He skimmed the decrypt documentation, found the thinness of the paper sheets interesting, an apparent conservation effort and handed it back. "Now that is one excellent action tracking system," he said. Wheels turned inside Tony's mind as he mentally peered into the vault. That room hopefully held the prize sought by Project Cigar. "Well Petra, I'm not sure how far back I want to go but I would like each day to review the most current day and a prior day's German Navy decrypts, continually working backwards in time while continuing to maintain currency. It was last September that the Royal Navy changed from Maritime Cypher Two to Three because it became clear that B-Dienst was breaking Number Two. Our governments are getting a little pissy with each other about finding the vulnerability the Germans have found, so this is both a political and technical topic. Anyway, all that aside, I guess I want to work my way back to July of 1941. That should give me some valuable insights."

Petra shook her head, "I'm not sure how long it will take to do that, some days we had more success decrypting their messages than others, but it will be a lot of material in any case." She turned to Molly, "Miss Lawson, please get the files the Commander needs, for yesterday and keep track of what he's seen so there's logical continuity."

Tony went to his desk and discussed some administrative details with Molly. She made a log sheet to track his progress and disappeared into the vault. Her natural brown hair was styled in a neat bun that he guessed would probably be ear length when let down. She had a certain charm about her that was subtly attractive and a bit younger, mid-twenties or so.

Petra took a short telephone call then turned to Tony, "As you finish up on each day's file, we'll bring you another."

"Perfect," said Tony.

"There's been some talk about many more Yanks coming to the Park to help," she put emphasis on the word help, "I don't think many here are looking forward to it, but you seem like a decent chap."

Tony smiled, "Well thank you Petra. We're not the ogres you may have heard about." They laughed.

"Where are you staying?" she asked.

"An attic room at Dr. Pearson's nearby. It was arranged by London through some mutual friend or something, but I'll be looking for a place to rent, which I'm sure won't be easy to find. If you know or hear of any, let me know. Pearson is on his own now, his wife of 50 years has passed, seems like a good chap, and enjoys the company. But, we're on a very different schedule."

"Right. There's a posting board in one corner of the canteen where people post lets and trades, check there. The personnel office also maintains some semblance of control over room and board agreements with the local owners and assignments, so check with them as well. Most everyone is living off base, finding a place to rent close isn't easy anymore."

"And what's to do in off time here?" he asked.

"Ah, well then, you'll find entertainment postings in the canteen as well. If you play an instrument, there's a couple quartets and they are forming a small orchestra," she said pausing for his response.

"Oh my God no, my musical skills were well proven to be unacceptable in high school," he said laughing.

She joined his laughter, "Perhaps some acting skills? We have a drama group that puts on skits and plays and they are quite good."

He shrugged, "I never tried acting, but it's something I might attempt if it looks like I'll have the time for it."

She smiled, "Right. Failing all that, they also post the cinema, sports and dance schedules. There's actually more to do than there's off time for it."

"Now we're talking, I can do those things," he said laughing. "Oh one small aside Petra, before I dive in here, how's the food in the canteen?" asked Tony.

"Right, well I'm not sure what your tastes are," explained Petra, "but we all find it rather plain, nothing posh, but satisfactory to most and it's open all day and night. Handy, yes?"

Tony nodded, "Very. I'm not a picky eater, my mother would not allow that. Your choice was to eat what's on the table or not. No other options."

"My mum was quite the same," she said with a smile.

3 A DANCE WITH MOLLY

Working closely with Molly was a pleasure. It was clear to both of them that they were attracted to each other. Her Scottish accent, bright wit, unpretentious and simple nature were all intriguing characteristics. It made their intermittent lunches and dinners an interesting break in long tedious days. They talked about music, films, books, their lives and, of course, Bletchley gossip. They began meeting intermittently with other Bletchley personnel after hours at Livingston's pub before retiring to their respective lodgings. Second Officer Petra Wilkinson had already shown some curiosity about their interactions and taking meals together frequently. Neither Tony nor Molly wanted to raise the ire of either Wilkinson or the base commander, Captain Hardcastle, so they agreed to make their pub meetings appear not to be prearranged. Oh sure, they both knew it wasn't the right thing to do under the circumstances, but the magnetism between them was proving stronger than their better judgement.

Tonight was a slow one at the pub. Tony was seated at the bar enjoying his first sips of a pint of half and half. Livingston's was a very old-fashioned local pub, plain but comforting. The dark hardwood bar had intricately trimmed molding and support columns. It looked to be over a hundred years old and had room for a dozen stools or so. Opposite the bar were a few small tables and some booths that ran along one wall. On one end of the room, near the oversized gray fieldstone fireplace, was a six by ten-foot area of slightly raised hardwood flooring that pub goers used for dancing. Thanks to the expansion of the staff at Bletchley, Livingston's seemed to burst at the seams on Friday and Saturday nights but this Monday night was relatively quiet.

Molly entered the pub, muttering about the weather, passed by the bar and said, "Shandygaff Doc if you please." Reginald Livingston had been given the nickname of Doc many moons ago by the locals, who poked fun by greeting him with "Doctor Livingston I presume." He was not related to the Doctor Livingstone of fame, but that was of no consequence to his hecklers having fun.

She put her heavy top coat, scarf and knit hat on a wall hook and sat next to Tony. "Good evening Commander," she said and took her first sip of a beer and ginger ale combination that Tony once tasted and quickly declared it to be a vile concoction.

"Good evening Molly, nice to see you," he said, admiring her rosy cheeks. They joined in the banter with a carpenter, a wood mill worker and two retired horse trainers at the bar. A lively discussion ensued about horse breeding, Hitler, eating horse meat, the collapse of France and the rising cost of lumber and scarcities of common household and food items. All that ended when the horsemen were served their vegetable soup and dark bread. The radio on the mantle could now be heard more prominently; the announcer was finishing a news report about President Roosevelt signing an Executive Order requiring all aliens to register with the government, which had apparently become a political hot potato. After a brief weather report, the announcer introduced the start of a music program, "Ladies and gentleman, we begin with Glenn Miller's new hit from the movie Sun Valley Serenade, Chattanooga Choo-Choo."

"How about a dance, Molly?" asked Tony.

"Lovely," said Molly wasting no time to leave her stool. "I really know nothing about carpentry or horses, they are such a bloody bore," she whispered in his ear as they began dancing. They laughed quietly. The fireplace warmed their bodies and after three drinks their minds mellowed and inhibitions faded. The third round wasn't intended, but one of the horsemen insisted on buying a round for the bar. They stayed on the dance floor talking softly.

"Think the Captain would approve of this, Molly?" he asked rhetorically then realized how silly that question was.

She chuckled, "He bloody well would not but what he doesn't know won't hurt him."

Since Tony arrived in A Block, they had been trying to maintain the type of relationship expected of two work mates. Tonight, dancing closely, they were coming to the realization that this was futile effort. "I don't know if it's the beer, but you feel wonderful," he said, holding her snugly and admiring the flicker in her eyes of the burning fireplace logs as they turned.

Tony felt her press more firmly against him and place her hand on the back of his neck. She said nothing, but moved her head from his shoulder and looked deeply into his eyes for several seconds. He put his arm more completely around her waist and tucked their clasped hands between their shoulders. He felt their lips just barely touch once as they danced. Then they touched again. Then their lips began to brush more frequently. Both of them knew full well that they were now overtly and shamelessly teasing one another. When they just could not stand it any longer, their mouths came together for a lingering animated kiss.

"We're such fools Tony, I'm just glad there's nobody here from Bletchley" she whispered.

"We can't be so daring in public," he said with a chuckle.

Molly took a deep breath and whispered in his ear with an endearing giggle, "Quite. We'll sort it out." They grinned into each other's eyes.

His mind was reeling, "Even though I'm on my own at the cottage, I don't feel it's a wise thing."

"Right. A house warming is out of the question, but I have an idea, if you find it acceptable," she said enthusiastically. "Several years ago I met a former school chum and her husband at Bowman's Inn, a bit north of here, near Castlethorpe. It's not likely that anyone at Bletchley ever heard of it and it's just lovely." Her eyes were now sparkling.

He squeezed her hand, "It sounds wonderful. Can you get free this weekend?"

"I've worked so many straight days, I'm sure I can get off Friday and Saturday, we can go there Friday," she said beaming.

"Great!" he whispered as he held her close.

4 BAD NEWS

The Following Monday
Bletchley Park

The scant light of the new day was barely in transition from a moonless night. The cold damp air was biting Tony's nose and ears as he hurried along. Walking at a fast pace helped minimize the effects of Jack Frost. The 20-minute walk to the Bletchley gate from his quaint off-base cottage seemed intolerably long. Winter weather in England reminded him of his childhood days in Maine and also of winter walks from Harvard University Commons to class. It seemed like just a few days ago that Christmas was approaching and he was at the Main Navy building on Constitution Avenue in DC reading his urgent orders to London. His mind also wandered through last weekend's memorable first rendezvous with Molly Lawson. Thoughts of her were mingling with analyzing German high command and submarine communications. Project Cigar documents were, as usual, lurking in the subconscious; simple sounding task, but onerous to execute, not to mention a political danger zone.

Memories of last weekend with Molly warmed his thoughts as he plodded through the cold dawn. He smiled as he thought of how they missed breakfast after keeping each other awake most of Friday night. He was anxious to see her again this morning for the first time since their last embrace outside the inn Saturday afternoon. They returned to their quarters separately in the interest of discretion.

As the distance to Bletchley's gate shortened, he narrowed his focus on the task of analyzing the last two days of decrypted German messages. Determining the security of encrypted U.S. and U.K. convoy communications grew ever more important with Hitler's acceleration of U-boat construction and the directly proportional increase in wolfpack sizes and numbers. Their growing submarine force was sure to have greater success in sinking or damaging shipping from the U.S. bound for Great Britain. He always used his commute to work to plan his day. But, this day would not go as planned.

He merged in with the other early risers moving through the Bletchley gate, ID cards held forward for the sentry's inspection. The light shining down from the top of the sentry house eerily highlighted puffs of hoary breath as each person passed by. He headed directly for the "mansion." He was anxious to feel the warmth from the radiator and a cup of hot tea in the austere desk area assigned to him in the mansion garage loft. He would much prefer good strong black coffee but he was in Rome and at the mercy of the Romans. The simple fact was that after less than a month in England, he'd come to appreciate tea, as well as room temperature beer. It was a far cry from the vast creature comforts to which he had become accustomed in Washington, DC.

Tony stuffed his gloves in his bridge coat pocket and hung it along with his hat and scarf on the unfinished pine wood clothes tree standing in the corner. He rubbed his hands rapidly to restore circulation to his tingling fingers, grabbed his oversized ceramic British military issue mug, blew the dust out of it and walked down the steps. Captain Hardcastle's Yeoman was heading toward him as he came to the little table between file cabinets that was being used as a tea mess for the analytical personnel laboring in the garage. "Good morning Petty Officer," said Tony while filling his cup to the brim with steaming Earl Grey from one of two oversized white ceramic pots adorned with hand painted English roses and ivy vines. Since both pots were identical, one simply chose plain black tea, the pot always on the left, or Earl Grey, on the right, confirmed by the fragrance from the spouts.

"Good morning sir," said the Petty Officer, "Captain Hardcastle wishes to see you at 0830. I'll be bringing your daily message and reading file shortly." Tony nodded with a smile, went back up the stairs and settled into his chair. He quickly downed half the mug of tea which warmed his core. Tony plunged into the thick pile of documents in the reading file when it was delivered. He caught up on yesterday's intelligence summaries and other correspondence. It was a clumsy organizational implementation, having two offices, but it was the Captain's way of keeping a closer eye on him than would be possible if Tony worked exclusively in A block.

A summons from Hardcastle was more likely a matter of concern than of little consequence and it nibbled at his concentration on the read file. They may be in navies that are friendly to each other but his professional relationship with Hardcastle was an entirely different story. He spent an hour going through the daily update reading, stood to stretch, then went to the one window of the loft and pulled aside the blackout curtains. He peered out into what was now the dull early morning light of another overcast day. Outside his window was of a bee hive of activity. The Park's workforce was pouring in steadily going hither and yon to the many huts and buildings on the estate to tackle this day's critically important intelligence work.

A shiver ran down Tony's spine at the first glance of Captain Hardcastle's grim face. Tony offered a proper military greeting and sat in the chair Hardcastle pointed at. Tony speculated about the gentleman that was seated next to him in a tweed coat, holding a bowler in his lap. Hardcastle's weathered face bore a glare that was far colder than ever before. The Captain had been difficult to deal with at best but this had promise of being worse than that. Hardcastle drew a deep breath, his brow furrowed deeply and his bushy gray eyebrows raised then lowered as he took on a stern scowl. He focused his pale blue-gray eyes intently on Tony, "Lieutenant Commander Romella, you are here on a very serious matter. This is Inspector Hale of Scotland Yard." Tony's heart skipped a beat; he felt his face flush despite not knowing why.

The inspector turned to face Tony with wide eyes that seemed to be boring deeply, "Sir, may I ask where you were last night?"

Tony thought briefly, "In A Block, I worked until 9pm or so. Why?"

"Right," said Hale, "is that normal for a Sunday? Can you think of anyone who can vouch for your presence through the course of the evening?"

"Well sure it's normal, we take a day or two off only now and then, but the war doesn't stop, so we work every day. And yes, Second Lieutenant Petra Wilkinson and Molly Lawson can vouch for me. They were there when I got to A Block and were still there when I left," Tony replied, feeling anxiety building rapidly. "What's going on?

"Right," said Hale, "and where did you go after you left A Block?"

"I walked directly from the Park to Livingston's Pub, a small detour on the way to my cottage," said Tony.

"How long did you stay at the pub?" asked Hale.

"Perhaps an hour, not more, then I went home." Tony searched their faces alternately, "Please, tell me what this is about."

Hale scribbled notes on a piece of paper that he had carefully folded to fit in his palm. "Right, now sir, did you meet or spend time with anyone in particular at the pub?"

"Nobody."

"Nobody?" asked Hardcastle in a pretentious tone.

"Nobody, well of course there were some people at the pub that I spoke to while I was there, nothing other than regular pub banter," said Tony.

Hale nodded, "Did you speak with anyone in particular? Have any arguments with anyone?"

Tony shook his head, trying unsuccessfully to restrain his disgust with the cat and mouse game in progress, "Why don't you just ask me what you're looking for Inspector? Nothing of significance happened last night. I sat on a stool, drank a pint, chatted a bit and went home. That's it!"

Captain Hardcastle leaned forward on his elbows, flashing the bands of four wide gold stripes on his navy blue uniform sleeves, "You can bloody well expect we'll find out if all that is true, Lieutenant Commander!"

Hale turned to Hardcastle and interrupted, "Give us some patience, both of you. Now tell me Commander, did you speak at length with any women while you were at the pub last night?"

"I'm sure I spoke with every man and the one woman that was in the pub last night. There weren't that many people and we all know of each other from the Park, somewhat, or from the pub, but I have no idea what their names were." Captain Hardcastle began nodding with a smirk, as though he had caught a fox in the hen house. "Captain," interrupted Tony, "There's nothing inappropriate about that."

Hardcastle came to his feet, "I know what is appropriate, and I also know that you and Miss Lawson most probably spent time together last weekend. That's bloody well true, yes?"

Inspector Hale shot Hardcastle a chilling look, "Please Captain, allow me to follow my line of questioning without interruption." Hale turned to Tony, "Was Miss Lawson at the pub when you were there last night?

"No sir, she was not. The last time I saw her in the pub was last week," said Tony.

"And you left the pub and went directly home alone last night?"

"Yes, sir," said Tony.

"Right. Now did you see or speak with Miss Lawson anytime, anywhere, after you left the pub?" asked Hale.

Tony shrugged his shoulders, "No sir, I did not."

Inspector Hale hesitated a moment and said, "Commander, I am sorry to inform you that she was murdered last night on her way home from the base and you, Mr. Romella, through your close working and personal association with her, are thus implicated in this case."

Tony could not hold the tears back; they began flowing steadily down his cheek while he wrestled with powerful emotions building inside him. He tried to speak but couldn't form the words. He took a handkerchief from his pocket to wipe his eyes. He tried to speak again, but no words found their way out until he leaned forward and buried his face in his hands. "This is, just, oh my God, impossible."

Hale paused a bit, then continued, "Lieutenant Commander, do you know if anyone was angry with her? Did she have any enemies, jealous lovers or suitors, anything of the like?"

Tony felt a wave of nausea trying to sweep through his body but maintained composure. He had very quickly come to care for Molly a great deal during these past couple weeks at the Park. When he was sure he wasn't going to lose his morning tea he said, "This is awful, a nightmare." His body slumped in the chair as though someone let the air out of him.

"I must ask you again," said Hale, "do you know of anyone that might be of interest? Former boyfriends? Anyone at all?"

"Inspector, that young lady was liked by everyone. Everybody! I don't know of anyone who was angry with her for any reason and she never mentioned anything about men in her life, past or present," said Tony. There was a seeming long pause with dead silence while Hale reviewed some notes. Tony's mind reeled then seized on something, "Come to think of it," said Tony, "about a week ago she did mention to one of the ladies that came into the office in A Block that there was a man who had annoyed her at the pub. The other woman, I have forgotten her name, said she too had found that same man Molly described as being a bit much, but Molly never mentioned it to me directly. And for the record, I did not murder Molly or have anything to do with it. I absolutely did not!"

Inspector Hale nodded, put his notes away, bid a good morning and left Hardcastle's office. When the inspector closed the door behind him, the Captain focused his gaze on Tony, "You are a risk to the good order and discipline of Bletchley Park and if you won't leave voluntarily, I will request the Ministry of Defense to have you transferred out presently."

Tony's stomach cramped, his face reddened and his ears began to burn. His mind ran wide open as he rejected one possible response after another, each being less tactful than the last. The words of his direct superior and good friend, the U.S. Naval Attaché London, Commander Bill Taylor, echoed through his head, cautioning Tony to do whatever was necessary to maintain a professional relationship with the venerable Captain Hardcastle so that neither of Tony's missions at Bletchley would be compromised or degraded. Hardcastle was waiting, tapping his fingers on his desk, maintaining an intent look in expectation of a reply. Tony swallowed hard, "Captain, as you know sir, Livingston's Pub is a place many Bletchley personnel frequent, officer, enlisted and civilian."

"Bloody foolish Yank you are Lieutenant Commander Romella," bellowed Hardcastle, seeming to stop in mid-thought. To say that the Captain was furious and frustrated with Tony's presence would be an understatement. Tony could see that plainly in Hardcastle's eyes and body language. The Captain stood up, "Yanks fraternizing with British women from this command just is not acceptable." Tony was speechless. They had covered this ground before and Tony thought it had been settled. Hardcastle began pacing back and forth, "I don't know how you Yanks think you can come in here and bring your bad habits with you, but in my command you bloody well will not get involved with any of our women. Their husbands and sweethearts are not here for the most part and have not been for some time. They have mostly come from modest backgrounds and are vulnerable to your bribery of money and trinkets." Hardcastle dropped into his chair.

Tony nodded, "Your point is well taken sir, but I have not violated the agreement we made on my first day here. I cannot deny or hide my life's good fortune. Granted, it gives me more resources than most and I have been generous, but that is beside the point. I am here because I am a naval intelligence officer that has been working on German Navy intelligence projects in Washington since the beginning of the war. The pending German implementation of their Triton crypto system threatens to cut off the source of ULTRA intelligence about the German submarine force to both of our countries. Our countries are cooperating fully to maintain our ability to read those messages. The German cryptanalysts have already had successes against Merchant shipping cyphers which our countries use jointly and threatens the logistic lifeline the U.S. is sending to your country. You and I are on the same side of all these challenges, sir. And directly to the point of fraternization, Molly was of an equivalent rank of a military officer, which was within the guidelines. Sir, I am merely here to ensure that the U.K. and the U.S. get full advantage of the joint resources of our two countries in the pursuit of sources of critical intelligence and the security of our merchant marine communications. That, sir, is the only agenda I have. And, Captain, just for the record, and I say it with utmost emphasis, Molly was not known to have any attachments and I damn sure did not murder her!"

Hardcastle scowled, "Perhaps we don't need help. The analysts, cryptanalysts and mathematicians here are quite capable of doing their work without the likes of you yanks, despite what Mr. Churchill and Mr. Roosevelt might think."

Tony sighed and studied Hardcastle's eyes, "Sir, let's look at the situation you and I are facing. We both have our orders. Our governments have brought us together on a military mission in a horrible war. Is it not our duty to make the best of it despite our differences?"

Hardcastle shook his head, face now ruddy, "I am still in command of this bloody park and I am responsible for the people in it."

"Yes sir, I understand and respect that very much. I only ask that you expect nothing more from me than you expect from any British officer." Hardcastle bristled and sat up tall in his chair. With his typical cold expression and tone he said, "Well there we have it, Lieutenant Commander Romella, you have stepped across the bloody line and I'm pulling the U.K. welcome mat at Bletchley out from under you. Your access to classified material here is suspended pending the Scotland Yard investigation. I expect you'll return to London promptly. When you leave this office, I presume you'll depart this building promptly. Your secrecy act privileges are suspended and you may not enter any other buildings in Bletchley Park. Dismissed."

5 THE DOCTOR CALLS

U.S. Naval Attaché Office
Grosvenor Square, London

"Good afternoon Captain, I'm sorry about this situation, I had no control over any of this," said Tony as he entered Captain Taylor's office and closed the door behind him.

Taylor nodded and motioned to Tony to have a seat, "It was best that you got out of there without any fuss. We sure didn't need Hardcastle to keep stewing over this and make more damn noise in the OPCEN and MOD. Washington is still negotiating details with the Brits to get more troops and resources into the country, Bletchley included. The less noise on this subject the better."

"Bill, I had absolutely nothing ..."

Taylor interrupted Tony, "I believe you, there's no question in my mind and it looks like MI5 believes you. I'm not sure why and they aren't sharing their reasons. The simple fact is, they aren't concerned about you at all. Thankfully, there's no push to send you back to DC. I heard that may not be the first murder or personal security issue up there, but that's just a rumor. I hope that Scotland Yard soon figures out that you're not involved in this instance so we can get on with things. Until they do, I'll have no trouble keeping you busy here. We have no idea how long this will go on and MI5 had nothing to offer. Anyway, how are you holding up? I'm sure it's a shock. I hear you two had become close."

"I'm doing ok Bill. How did you hear that?"

"A little bird, Tony."

"Well, I have to say that her murder has just been unthinkable and a terrible shock. And yes we were getting involved. It's hard to get her out of my mind. We only just started seeing each other romantically, but I cared a great deal about her."

Bill nodded, "By the way, I arranged a flat for you to call home while you're in London. Frankly, it's a safe-house the Brits loaned us. It's not very big or fancy, I checked it out, austere is a good description, but an easy commute. It's a short walk from the Wembley Park tube station. It's yours for the duration of your tour of duty with the embassy. I'm sure you don't fancy the rack in the embassy basement Visiting Officer Quarters. Besides, the embassy needs those temporary quarters for other short term visitors. Bear in mind, you're involved in a Yard murder investigation and this safe house belongs to the Brits."

"Thanks Bill, I get your drift. Now, what do you have for me while I'm considered Jack the Ripper?" asked Tony.

"It's hardly trivial make-work Tony, we've got something hot that popped up and we can use some help on it. The classification of this information is Top Secret. MI5 thinks there is a German spy active in the greater London area and you can use your imagination and hear Bletchley in that. The Brits obviously want to locate and capture him and, with some luck, turn him," said Taylor.

"What makes them think this? Are they sure it's a German? And male? " asked Tony.

"They aren't sharing everything with me right now, I know, but they did ask if I had any ideas that might help. They are giving me what I need to know when I need to know it, but they've given me a hell of a lot. They said they have intercepted a few manual Morse messages using what they feel are agent protocols on short-wave radio frequencies. The signal strength and other characteristics reported by Morse intercept operators indicate it's a ground-wave signal. I'm not sure what that means, but I know you do. So, given your experience with ham radio and signal direction finding systems, I thought you might have something to offer."

Tony nodded, "Oh, this is interesting. Bill, I would take a Morse intercept operator's assessment of the signal any day. I can tell you, a radio operator has a sixth sense about signals that's rarely wrong. There's a world of difference in the solid, booming sound of a ground-wave signal that's relatively close and one that's bounced off ionospheric layers due to notable distance from the receiver. Do the Brits have any direction finder bearings on these signals?"

"They said they have, I'm quoting here, lines of bearing that run generally through central London. A Brit signal intercept site recently reported lines of bearing on three transmissions, over the course of several days. Their preliminary assessment tells them the transmitter is possibly located near London, but they explained that it's not conclusive since the transmitter could be located anywhere along the lines of bearing. All that makes some sense to me, but I'm sure perfect sense to you."

"It does indeed Bill, but they probably won't want me involved."

"Oh ye of little faith. I related to MI5 in a meeting this morning that you have had some experience as a ham operator and were involved in the planning and operations of our Morse intercept and direction finding network. They didn't even flinch. Which is why I say they know you're not involved with Molly. Long story made short, they are making a portable DF set from a Telefunken short wave radio. They want you to set it up in your flat in hopes you'll be able to get line bearings on this guy that will provide cross-bearings to those from the DF site near Bletchley and help locate the transmitter. I have a folder they dropped off after that meeting. Looks like it documents all the times and frequencies he's used so far, along with some other technical details MI5 shared.

Tony skimmed through the folder. "This rota, the transmission schedule info, will be very helpful. Interesting that they are using a modulated continuous wave signal and sending the messages at very high speed after contact is made. Probably using a device to record hand sent Morse, then they play it back through the transmitter at a high speed. That'll make it hard to catch him, or her, since they're not on the air long. I would say, off the top of my head, looking at these times of day and frequencies, they're probably transmitting to someone in western France. I'll do some research and make some calculations to confirm that."

Captain Taylor perked up, "Oh that's a fascinating observation. MI5 has a suspicion that this guy is reporting back to a handler on Admiral Dönitz's intelligence staff. As you know, Dönitz just happens to have his HQ in Kernevel."

Tony nodded, "Yes, just south of the port of Lorient on the west coast of France."

They probably have more intel on all this than they have shared, but that's fine," said Bill. "They seem to give us what we need when we need it."

"I agree Bill. They probably have some sensitive HUMINT or they've gotten some clues from decrypted messages to or from this agent. This is interesting, real interesting. You know? This might tie in with the merchant shipping cipher system security problem. If this agent has a source of merchant shipping info of any sort, it would be something near and dear to Dönitz," said Tony.

Captain Taylor shuffled through some notes on the right side of his desk and found the one he wanted, "Now, let's talk about a weekend assignment that you will find a little more like fun, albeit a rather snooty gathering of attachés," said Bill with a grin forming on his face, "I have to go to Portsmouth; I'll be back next Monday afternoon. This will give you a chance to hobnob with some aristocracy and attachés from other countries." Bill handed Tony the note. "You can make the call to confirm."

Tony scanned the note and looked at Bill with a side glance. "Is there another layer to this?"

Bill laughed, "I can't understand why you would think that. You're not going to bring up that little white lie I had to tell you in Moscow are you?"

Tony laughed, "Uh, yeah, I sure am."

"Seriously Tony, this one you'll enjoy. Lady Watson invited some attachés to her estate for a Saturday afternoon tea party, dinner that night and activities planned Sunday morning for those who can stay over. She puts on quite a soirée. Feel free to stay over if she invites you to do so and if you are so inclined. I have already given my regrets but I told her you may be able to attend and represent me."

"Aye, aye sir," Tony said with a smile. "Tell me about this Lady Watson."

"Lady Inga Watson is the widow of a Royal Army Brigadier General who had a fatal heart attack in Sweden, around 1938. She is very wealthy on her own, let alone the Brigadier, may he rest in peace. She's from a wealthy Swedish family that made their money in shipping and ship building with fish processing plants thrown in for good measure."

"Intriguing," said Tony.

Bill nodded, "The general was the son of Lord Percival Watson, who had amassed a sizeable wealth from farm equipment manufacturing. The general had several attaché assignments during his career so she has a soft spot in her heart for the attaché corps. She entertains frequently for benefit of the diplomats and attachés here in London. She knows people from all over the world, stays connected with them and is a good source of gossip. Bring some back. This is a social affair to be sure, but it's also an important event for the attaché office. Don't take it lightly. She's nice to look at, I might add."

"Aha! I knew there was another layer to this and it boils down to scuttlebutt. OK, I'll be suitably attentive and on my best behavior," Tony said wryly.

6 A MAJOR INTRODUCTION

Havenwood—the Estate of Lady Inga Watson
Suburb of London

The embassy driver slowed the sedan as he neared a gated entrance that stood proudly in the center of a thick green five-foot hedge that ran for seemingly a mile or so along a narrow winding country road. As they turned into the entrance, an attendant swung the sturdy wooden gate open. Tony noted that the wood of the gate looked relatively new and that there were wood fixtures attached to it that mated with notably rusted iron ones anchored in the stone columns on either side. This was evidence that the wrought iron of the gate had been donated to the war effort to be smelted and become part of a tank or ship. Tony was in a bit of awe as they proceeded down the estate entrance road. The fine gravel of the road crunched noisily under the tires as he drank in the latent natural beauty of the naked limbs and branches of shrubs and trees that embellished the pathway. The road ran about a hundred yards to a wide circle in the front of a huge three story fieldstone mansion. Each side of the road was lined with tall stately trees that had over-arching branches the formed lush canopies in the summer. A wide lawn stretched out from either side of the road. The lawn on the right side butted up against a forest, the other seemed to roam hill and dale for acres.

He learned that Lady Watson had not yet returned from a London appointment when her staff greeted Tony and the other guests as they arrived at the mansion. The greeters had umbrellas at the ready due to a light drizzle that had descended on the estate. Everyone was ushered to their rooms as they arrived, to freshen up and prepare for the first event of this weekend's festivities—a formal afternoon tea.

Tony entered his room on the second floor. Wide rustic hardwood planks creaked beneath his feet. His eyes flew immediately to the huge canopied four-poster bed that nearly filled the room. The matching fabric of the canopy and comforter were stunning in their design and workmanship and, he thought, not accidentally blue with gold trim—U.S. Navy colors. On the outside wall there was a window with blackout curtains drawn back. It revealed a grand view of the sprawling back area of the estate, illuminated by the dull light of a heavily overcast day. A small fireplace gave the room both visual warmth and heat. The burning logs provided a soft pulsating golden glow of light as well as random snaps and pops that delighted the ear of a northeasterner. The mild smell of oak carbon and the dancing flame tips on the logs reminded him of Maine. One of his morning chores as a teenager during the winter months was stocking the log bin next to the big fireplace in their living room and removing the prior day's ashes. His eyes turned next to a modest but elegantly sculptured dark cherry corner desk where a handwritten schedule of events was carefully laid. It gave details for this afternoon's formal tea, this evening's dinner-ball and tomorrow morning's breakfast, complete with menus and proper dress for each activity. Lady Watson had her standards for afternoon tea, at least for such an occasion as this. She provided hand written notes to the ladies and gentlemen on attire. Tony imagined that the ladies would not be going light on finery and therefore so would go the men. There was a splendid mix of efficient military order and the air of polite civil formality in it all. He sat on the edge of the bed, which seemed excessively high. He couldn't resist laying back and sank deep into a down comforter. Closing his eyes he wondered if it was fair that he should be enjoying such pleasures while such a brutal war was raging across the channel. He wondered how and why Molly, sweet Molly, met her demise and if he would ever set foot onto Bletchley Park again. His free-wheeling mind had managed somehow to shut down and allowed him to drift off peacefully, until his nap was interrupted by the rich peal of the miniature grandfather clock centered between unlit white candles in brass holders on the mantle. There was exactly one hour before high tea.

Unpacking, freshening his shave, shining shoes and getting into his dress blues ate up 50 minutes. He inspected himself in the long mirror mounted on the inside of the left hand door on the impressive cherry armoire. Tony was anxious to finally meet Lady Watson and her guests. He joined others moving down the carpeted semi-circular fruit wood grand staircase and took his place in a receiving line that led down a short L-shaped hallway. The attachés of several countries were resplendent in their sharply pressed dress uniforms. Their ladies wore tea-length dresses of varying color and design, complete with gloves. Everyone introduced themselves, chatted and laughed as though they were fast friends. There was an innate comradery in this circle of people that was interesting, pleasant and a bit surreal. As the reception line moved toward the large room where high tea was being held, he amused himself by conjuring a mental vision of Lady Watson. He patiently awaited the first glimpse of his hostess now perhaps 15 feet away, hidden behind a doorway. He refined his mental picture of her as he neared the doorway. He imagined her to be a large-framed and perhaps rotund lady about 60 years old, standing 5'5" with less than notable looks punctuated by a forced smile, graying blonde hair and Nordic blue eyes. As he passed through the doorway, Lady Watson finally came into sight. He was partly right, she was large-framed, had blonde hair imaginatively piled on her head to perfection and had dazzling blue eyes. Otherwise, the tiny waist of her lacy green and white form fitting gown showed she was athletically trim. She appeared to be 50 years old at most and at least 5'10". The design of her gown accentuated her curves. Finally, he was next in line. As the butler announced him, Lady Watson stretched out her hand with an elegance that must have taken weeks to perfect and gave a smile that melted the polish on his shoes. She could pass for Lana Turner's older sister, he thought. Her Swedish accent was unmistakable as she greeted him, "Welcome to Havenwood Commander Romella, I must ask Captain Taylor why he has kept you hidden."

Tony took her hand gently, "Thank you Lady Watson, I am very pleased to meet you. I have only recently arrived in the U.K. so the Captain is innocent of any charges," he said with a smile.

She surprised Tony by engaging a very firm grip. The texture of her long white lace glove was surely a great contrast to the soft hand inside. "Since this is your first visit to Havenwood Commander, please don't be bashful, make yourself at home. My staff is at your disposal. And please do save us a dance this evening."

"It will be my pleasure," he said. With that, she turned her gaze to the next couple in line and he moved forward toward the tables elegantly set with silver, ornately decorated china and faceted crystal goblets accented with rose colored stems. Place cards were at each of the tables, all set for four. Tony wandered around the tables, reading the name cards, taking note of the name, ranks, position titles and countries represented. Aside from British military officers and other civilian guests, Lady Watson invited attachés from Australia, Canada, New Zealand, Russia, Spain, Sweden and Switzerland. He applied mental gimmicks he mastered at Harvard to remember multiple and diverse facts so that he could later recall and log all the attendees. When he completed his tour of the tables, he followed the others out onto the oblong solarium that ran parallel with the reception room. The ladies were gathering at one end to greet each other and gossip while the officers and civilian gentlemen went to the opposite end to smoke, drink pink gin and exchange war stories, pleasantries, humor and outright lies. Tony mingled and joined the conversations until the faint tinkle of a hand bell summoned them to their tables for tea and several choices of exquisite miniature sandwiches.

Later that afternoon, following the tea extravaganza and another short nap, Tony changed into an old khaki uniform and boots. The thick woods he saw through the bedroom window made him yearn for a stroll through them. He liked walking in the pine forests in Maine near his childhood home. He noted the drizzle had subsided, wrapped his neck with a white silk scarf, bundled up in his bridge coat, lifted up the wide collar and set out to explore.

The quiet of the woods, dimly lit from a dusk sun behind a low cloud ceiling, was broken only by the crunch of his shoes on a horse path and sounds of nature. The rustle of small animals and the call of a bird announcing the day's end was subtle yet rich music. His breath billowed out foggy white from his mouth and nostrils and the cold air numbed his nose and ears. The solitude allowed his mind to explore the circumstances at Bletchley and always in the back of his mind, there was Molly. As he walked briskly along a path bordered by barren trees and evergreens, he could not shut out the vision of Molly's smile and gentle personality. The shock of what was happening to him—and what may be in store—sank deep into his soul. Tony paused to lean back against a large oak trunk and closed his eyes to relive his last moments with Molly. A tear formed in each of his eyes and rapidly came to feel like piercing icicles.

When he returned from the walk, he discovered that a decanter of brandy had been placed on a small table outside his door, of which he took full advantage. Although only marginally tired from the long walk in the woods, the tall brandy he savored while taking a hot bath relaxed him to the point that a nap came easily.

Tony awoke abruptly under the down comforter on the four-poster bed. The chiming of the mantle clock interrupted the mental meanderings of light sleep. There was a scant glow in the room from the dregs of the last two logs he put in the fireplace. The embers provided enough soft light for him to see the hands on his watch when it was tilted toward the glow. He quickly came to full consciousness, realizing he had slept through dinner and that he only had a half hour to prepare for tonight's chamber music and dance. He immediately began worrying about how to explain this faux pas. His mind sorted the two obvious options, offer apologies before asked or wait until Lady Watson inquires. Neither seemed acceptable. It wasn't like him to stumble socially, but he had and he was unhappy about it.

The splendor of the ladies in their gowns and gloves, officers in their dress uniforms graced the great hall of Havenwood. Tony arrived just as the guests were being seated for the small concert that would precede the dance. The chamber quartet's selections were soothing and kept Tony's thoughts mostly occupied. Mostly because sitting in back of Lady Watson was a distraction. Especially with her perfume drifting intermittently back to him. It was light in fragrance but enchanting, like spring lilacs. Although she smiled at him and nodded politely when they were seating for the concert, he could sense subtleness in her smile and eyes which, in his guilt, conveyed a quiet displeasure. Perhaps he was just imagining. His late arrival had precluded any opportunity for conversation with her, or anyone, for that matter. After an hour of Bach and Mozart, the quartet took their bows and departed. Everyone retired to the solarium for cocktails and conversation. Meanwhile, the Havenwood staff hurriedly prepared the hall for dancing. Of course, Tony had to explain to several guests how he had come to miss dinner and found it no less embarrassing each time. The ladies stayed on their husband's arms for this trip to the solarium and added color to the chatter.

Lady Watson was circulating from couple to couple, engaging in small talk. She wandered over to Tony as he turned to leave his chat with the Spanish attaché. "Well, good evening Commander," she said, catching his attention from behind, "So gracious of you to join us." The tiniest hint of a grin revealed the playfulness of her scolding.

"Good evening Lady Watson, 'tis entirely my great honor," he said.

"And what pray tell kept us from my fine table?" she asked with an impish look, taking obvious delight in twisting his tail.

"Brandy and a hot bath, if you must know," he said, blushing. Tony felt his ears get red as his mind rambled. A couple in back of him couldn't help but overhear and chuckled, adding to his embarrassment.

"That was unfair of me, I'm sorry to be so forward," she said with a wide grin. "Don't forget, save us a dance, yes?"

"Certainly ma'am."

"Quite sir. My neighbors will soon be arriving. Their daughter, Gwyn, loves to dance. Perhaps you will give her the pleasure of a dance as well."

Tony smiled, "Of course ma'am."

Lady Watson paused, "You do waltz, don't you?"

"Yes Ma'am," he said, thinking how valuable last winter's dance lessons had become.

"Splendid. There will be nothing else this evening but waltzes. Do you enjoy them?" she asked.

"Yes Ma'am, waltz music is one of my favorites."

Lady Watson's eyes widened slightly as she saw something taking place inside the soon-to-be ballroom. "Please excuse me," she said and left to give her attention to the final preparations inside.

Tony turned his attention back to the guests. A brute of a man with a woman half his size approached and thrust his hand out, "Major Grischa Kiminko, Russian Army," he barked as he grabbed Tony's hand with a crushing grip, "Please to meet my wife, Nastasiya."

"Lieutenant Commander Tony Romella, U.S. Navy," said Tony returning the powerful grip, "Pleasure meeting you both." He nodded smartly to each of them as he catalogued the Major's distinguishing characteristics and chest full of colorful medals. Nastasiya's radiant green eyes were a contrast to a lack of expression and a pale yellow formal gown.

"Are you a new to London?" asked Grischa as he ran his fingers through his gray hair. "Yes sir," said Tony, "it has been just a few weeks now," he said.

"Are you, what you call, a black shoe, a ship driver?" Grischa asked with a grin, obviously pleased with himself for demonstrating his knowledge of U.S. Navy jargon.

"I am a line officer major, but I have spent only my first year in the Navy at sea, on the battleship Maryland," Tony replied, "I drive desks now."

Grischa laughed heartily, "I would rather be driving tanks, but my country and comrade general think London is better for me. How long is your assignment?"

"I don't know, as long as they wish it to be," said Tony with a shrug."

Grischa's eyes bored into Tony's, "Ah, you are with the embassy, da?"

Tony was now wishing he found answers that didn't lead down this path, "Oh yes, I am assigned to the embassy, under Commander Taylor."

Grischa and Tony ping-ponged questions back and forth on a wide range of topics, cleverly poking and prodding. The cat and mouse game was interrupted when a few members of Lady Watson's staff came to the solarium doorways and rang glass hand bells.

The chamber ensemble began playing a waltz which brought an orderly stream of guests from the solarium. Tony went directly to the bar in the back of the room to top off his champagne glass. All the others went directly to the dance floor. Tony watched Lady Watson glide across the hall to greet some new arrivals. She looked in Tony's direction and waved at him. She had her hand on the shoulder of an attractive young lady with a winsome smile and was whispering something to her as she beckoned Tony. He deduced that this was the neighbor's daughter, mid-twenties.

"Lord Thomas and Lady Guinevere Thornhill, please meet Lieutenant Commander Tony Romella, U.S. Navy from the American Embassy," said Lady Watson when Tony approached them. "Commander, these are my dear friends and neighbors, and this is their daughter Gwyn." Tony shook Thomas' hand, nodded to the ladies and traded polite words. Lord Thornhill's carefully pressed tuxedo and black bowtie was a contrast to the formal dress of the military officers. It was clear his Lordship had a military background owing to the line of miniature medals on his left breast. Lady Thornhill's full gown of earth-tones with copious white lace trimming seemed demure compared to Gwyn's bright red silk gown with a daringly low cut neckline. Gwyn had a model's face with creamy complexion and an infectious smile. She was alluring.

"I told the Thornhills about your plight, being at a dance with no partner," said Lady Watson, apparently relishing the embarrassment beginning to show on Tony's face, "and they have suggested that perhaps you would oblige Gwyn who is also without a dance partner tonight."

"The very least a gentleman could do," replied Tony. Gwyn sensed the onset of a situation where no one quite knew what to say next. She offered her arm to Tony and they hurried off to the dance floor.

"You may thank me now," said Gwyn, deep brown eyes glistening, as they swirled onto the floor.

"Oh, for the rescue?" asked Tony, "Yes, thank you!"

Gwyn smiled brightly, "Right. Whether you were rescued or placed into another form of extraordinary service remains to be seen, kind sir. I love, absolutely love to dance."

Tony laughed, "Are you threatening me with a bloody good time m'lady?"

She laughed, "Quite!"

After several waltzes in succession without leaving the dance floor, Tony and Gwyn learned a great deal about each other's lives, or as much as both would allow themselves to reveal at this point. She was not at all shy or reserved with a man she had just met, particularly with her parents present. She was, to his surprise, a greater delight than he anticipated. Tony was going to have to dig deep into his self-discipline to keep from being very attracted to her, despite her youth. Just the same, he was powerless to find a gentlemanly excuse to end the fun they were having. Regardless the energy he put into his waltzes, she followed without falter. The chamber ensemble took their first break. Tony excused himself to find the nearest water closet. When he returned to the great room he captured a flute of champagne from a circulating tray. Other trays making the rounds offered cucumber and butter sandwiches, crackers with goose liver pâté and other irresistible fare, all of which he sampled. The Thornhills had not yet returned to the great room, giving him time to think and decide whether to spend more time with Gwyn on the dance floor or retire to his room. As he was putting a cracker into his mouth the unmistakable voice of Lady Watson very close to his back broke his musings with a slight startle.

"Commander?" she said, "Oh, quite sorry to alarm you," she touched his shoulder and showed an exaggerated look of innocence.

Tony hurried his chewing to clear his mouth, "You caught me daydreaming, Lady Watson."

"Do tell, and please, please do call me Inga."

"In that case, please call me Tony, if you wish. I'm honored to share these blessings, they are such a contrast to the war at hand."

"Tony, that is precisely why I do this. We know not what tomorrow brings, thus we are wise to preserve our senses and sensibilities despite the bloody war."

"I for one certainly appreciate your efforts, expense and extraordinary hospitality. Thank you Inga."

She grinned, eyes twinkling and gave a brief curtsey. "The night is young, enjoy yourself. And I do indeed hope you chose to stay over for an early breakfast and horse riding after."

"How could I refuse?" he replied. "It's been quite a while since I've been on horseback. My family summered in the Maine mountains. Their log cabin was located next to a horse farm, where I met the farmer's son and became fast friends. We rode often and I helped tend to them. So, horses have always held a special place with me."

She smiled brightly, "Jolly good! It will be a pleasure to ride with you. The musicians are returning. Give us a few dances before Gwyn returns and commandeers you. Getting on with my neighbors are we?"

Lady Watson was as vigorous and graceful a waltz partner as Gwyn. It was as though she was not to be outdone. They swept across the floor of the great hall, winding their way through the uniforms and ball gowns. She kept a joyful smile on her face, proudly demonstrating her flawless waltz form, interjecting topics for small talk anytime their conversation seemed to lapse in the slightest. They exchanged childhood stories, reminiscences of their parents, musical preferences, favorite foods and military postings. She thought Humphrey Bogart performed brilliantly in The Maltese Falcon. Tony agreed but thought Peter Lorre also did a splendid job. And so it went. She kept him on the floor for several waltzes without a pause, right up to the next intermission. It had been many months since he had this much real fun. The infamous Lady Inga Watson was indeed nothing short of intriguing.

Sunday Morning

The butler escorted Tony to a large round table in the formal dining room, walls resplendent with detailed paneling adorned with medieval art and tapestries. Although the table would easily sit 12 comfortably, it was set beautifully for a sumptuous English breakfast for four. The Russian attaché and his wife had just been seated. The other guests for last night's soirée had returned to their respective homes. "Good morning Major and Mrs. Kiminko," said Tony with a sharp nod.

Nastasiya forced a smile and offered a phrase in Russian that, given the tone and delivery, was probably a morning greeting. The Major rose to shake Tony's hand, "Good morning Lieutenant Commander Romella, did you sleep well?" His English was nothing short of good, although heavily accented and as expected contained an occasional grammatical oddity.

Tony found his appointed seat opposite the Major. "Indeed I did Major, thank you for asking. I trust you both did as well. That was the first time I've slept in a four poster bed, with a canopy no less."

The Major nodded enthusiastically and translated for Nastasiya who was listening intently. She was wearing minimal makeup on her mildly attractive but expressionless face. Tony found her to be the most neutral personality he may have ever met, which conjured up a guarded curiosity. Just then, the oversized stained oak double doors to the dining room swung open. In bounded Lady Watson. She was dressed in her black riding britches, dark brown high boots, green blouse, fire red waist jacket and carrying a brown medium brimmed hat accentuated by a long white scarf. Everyone stood up, "Good morning my darlings," Inga greeted with a perky flair, "please sit down. I trust we had a good night's rest and all was tickety-boo throughout the evening?"

"Absolutely wonderful," said Tony noting how assimilated into British phraseology she had become. Lady Watson grinned at her guest's satisfaction and sat next to Tony.

Tony added, "Were it not for the butler's persistent knocking, despite my appetite, I would have been tempted to remain swallowed up in that toasty down bed for the remainder of the day."

"I think you exaggerate," said Lady Watson still smiling. "This is the whole of the party. Let's enjoy this meal shall we whilst still hot, but please, don't rush yourselves. The horses will wait patiently." Three young ladies in black and white uniforms with small white starched aprons immediately began serving each person individually from trays brought from cherry wood servers at the side of the room. The breakfast consisted of strong tea mixed with hot whole milk, thick steaming oatmeal, poached eggs on toast, kippers, blood sausage medallions, scones, soft butter and blackberry preserves. This hearty plate was apparently meant to fortify the guests for a long brisk ride. Tony dove into the meal with gusto.

Throughout breakfast, when Lady Watson wasn't carrying the conversation, the Major asked Tony questions about where in the U.K. he had been so far, what he saw that impressed him, what he studied in university and prior duty assignments. Eventually, the Major got around to asking Tony if he was involved in the issues involving intelligence sharing with Russia. Tony made sure he revealed nothing of importance and asked similar questions in return, which had the desired effect of throttling the Major from delving too deeply. The butler came into the dining room, whispered into the Major's ear and showed him into the drawing room off the dining room. When the Major returned, he made his apologies to Lady Watson, explaining that he had been recalled to his embassy.

"His name is Contender," Inga said as she handed reins of a large horse to Tony.

Tony looked him over and stroked his neck, "He's a big fellow and a beautiful chestnut."

Inga smiled, "He's very obedient yet he has a great deal of spirit."

They rode at a foot pace side by side toward the woods from the barn.

The crisp bite of early morning air was refreshing. He pulled the chin strap on his hat brim down and secured it under his chin.

"Right," she said loudly. He watched Inga's smile turn into a very devilish grin and with that, she whipped the reins lightly on her horse's rump, gently kicked her heels into her mount's ribs and picked up the pace of their ride to a fast trot. He rose high in the saddle and kept pace alongside her.

When they entered the path through the woods where he had ventured yesterday, she looked squarely at him, then used reins and heels on her horse again and took off at a fast gallop. He chased her through the winding path. The thuds of hooves and strong breathing of their horses was exciting. She could hear him right behind her and looked back only occasionally and very briefly. As they neared a stream, perhaps fifteen feet wide, she slowed to a trot again. Inga turned and looked back as they forded across a shallow section, "How's our bum doing? Have we had enough?"

He laughed heartily, "My bum is just fine."

"It's obvious that you have indeed ridden before. There's something interesting I'm going to show you just ahead," she said. "Farther upstream, the horses can rest and drink." He nodded. She soon stopped, dismounted, led her horse to the softly trickling stream and loosely tied the reins around the branch of a long dead trunk that lay next to the water. He did the same. "It's just a short walk up that little path," she said, pointing. "I come here often. There are ancient stones there that interest me to no end."

Perhaps thirty paces along a path roughly perpendicular to the stream, they came upon a clearing that had a circular arrangement of about a dozen grayish rectangular stones with peaks and corners that were once sharp but were now weathered and rounded. The flat faces were pocked and uneven. "A miniature Stonehenge," she said as she palmed one of the stone's surfaces.

"Amazing!" he said as he went to the center and turned slowly to admire each of the stones. The 20-foot circle seemed to be laid perfectly, although the stones no longer stood true, each was leaning in some random direction or, as with a few, had fallen. "This is truly amazing Inga. They do speak. If I only knew what they were saying. I really appreciate seeing this."

"I knew you would," she said.

"Has anyone researched and excavated?" he asked.

"We had a team of Doctoral candidates from Cambridge do some research out here a few years ago. Astronomers, anthropologists, mathematicians and the like, quite an interesting lot they were. Some artifacts were found within the circle that didn't seem to have meaning relative to the stones, but meaningful in some way. They did find the positions of certain stones to be significant regarding the equinoxes, like this one with a hole bored into it." She pointed to it. "They have documented their work well. I don't recall the details of their findings. You can review their documentation in the library when you're bored someday."

Tony walked to the most erect stone which, like the others, was about three feet taller than he, not counting the portion below ground. As he slowly smoothed his hand over the face of it he said, "I swear this thing has as many questions for me as I do of it."

"Quite. You're the first person to appreciate this so deeply. People usually just say how cold they are," said Inga, her bright eyes penetrating. "You must read all the things Cambridge wrote about them, then we'll sip brandy and opine what really happened among these stones in days of old."

7 DOCTORAL INTERCEPT

The Following Tuesday
U.S. Naval Attaché Office
London

"Sorry I couldn't see you yesterday, Tony. I spent a long day at the Admiralty and MOD. So, how was the weekend with Lady Watson?" asked Bill.

Tony grinned, "She wasn't what I expected Bill, not at all. Good looks, money, brains, one damn interesting lady!" He settled into the chair beside Bill's desk.

Bill laughed, "I just finished talking with her. You made a good impression also. She told me to bring you along for the next party. Oh, and the shit's hitting the fan on the Russian front. Did Kiminko show up?"

"Aye, but he left breakfast abruptly."

"I'm surprised he stayed overnight, things are tough back home. At least you got the opportunity to meet him and his wife. Glad you enjoyed your R&R," said Bill.

"What do you know about Major Kiminko?" asked Tony.

Bill nodded, "For one, he's almost shameless about pumping information out of you. He's been pulling GRU assignments for about ten years."

"Damn sure not a bashful guy about his mission, he made me uncomfortable a couple times," said Tony.

"Watch him, he's clever, I'm not sure what his agenda is, but over time I think he's trying to learn more about U.S. intelligence operations in the U.K. and our sentiments about intelligence exchange with Moscow. And, this is between us, OP20-g thinks there's a leak of ULTRA intelligence to Moscow. Kiminko may be tasked with finding out what we know about that."

"Good grief, Bill, does MI5 think it's a U.S. or U.K. leak?" asked Tony.

"Well, Tony, if I'm reading the tea leaves correctly, it's possibly MOD or higher. Hell, Kiminko may be the handler of the leaker, for all we know. But, all that is far from conclusive. By the way, what do you think of his wife?"

Tony collected his thoughts about her, "I, well, she seemed distant, sometimes I felt she was as cold as ice and although she hardly said anything, it was always in Russian and he translated. She seemed like she was very uncomfortable. I also get the gut feeling she's cunning as hell. Actually, she's one of those people that makes a chill go up your spine sometimes when she looks squarely at you."

"She strikes me the same way Tony. My guess is that she, like him, is a career NKGB officer. I'd almost bet a paycheck on that one. Say, how's progress on the direction finder set in your flat?"

"Up and running Sunday afternoon, but I haven't heard anything we're interested in. The DF display is a bit on the crude side but suffices for what we're doing.

"Good. Stay on it, sooner or later we'll get what we need on him," said Bill.

"That reminds me Bill, I've been thinking about how we refer to this target. We need an obscure term for unclassified reference that we both understand. Let's call him, uh, Doctor."

Bill smiled, "Doctor--good. I hope you can get something on the Doctor soon. I attended a meeting at Blenheim Palace yesterday and MI5 is extremely hot on this. They have a case number for him."

"Oh I bet they are quite interested," said Tony. "Blenheim Palace? Traveling in royal circles are we now boss?"

Bill smiled, "Not quite. After some damage to their HQ during the London blitz, MI5 moved the MI5 DG, their Director General, and some functions into Blenheim Palace at Woodstock. Some went into the former MGM building on Saint James Street. I don't get to the palace very often, most of my contacts are with the counter-espionage people at Saint James."

Tony nodded and smiled, "I'm getting envious of your job. Back to the Doctor, I'm spending a lot of time monitoring the short wave for him. Unless you object, I'm going to spend the vast majority of my time in the flat. The embassy Signal Corps guys came with some British civilian telephone techs and installed a telephone in the flat yesterday afternoon, ugly damn drab green one. At least we can conveniently and privately call each other." Tony wrote his name and telephone number on the Captain's scratchpad.

"I need to share some things with you before you go Tony, some Top Secret background on the Doctor.

"I figured they would eventually share more data about him," said Tony.

The Captain nodded, "Thanks to the diligence of the Bletchley folks, they've had good success with decrypting one of the low level coded messages to the Doctor. It's the oldest message that they have on file on this case, several months old they said. Turns out, it's the German Abwehr that is communicating with the Doctor. That mean anything to you?"

"Oh yes Bill, the Abwehr organization has a section that controls their espionage network," said Tony.

"Well, MI5 said that Bletchley's success with decrypting Abwehr messages to other agents has been incredibly valuable. It's been critical in their ability to identify and locate, they believe, every German agent in the U.K.. Except for the Doctor, of course, he's a horse of a different color.

The good part of it all is that MI5 has been able to turn most of their captives into double agents. Those that didn't turn, well, let's just say they were given new neck ties." Bill looked down at some notes he had scribbled, "MI5 also said that the communications patterns and frequencies don't fit the Abwehr communications profile for German agents seen to date," said Bill. He leaned back in his chair, which squeaked notably, "In fact, after that one early decrypted message, the Doctor and his control started using a different encryption system that we haven't been able to break into. It's a real puzzle and MI5 is concerned. It may mean the Germans realize their existing spy network codes were compromised and are responding accordingly, or just that the Doctor is now controlled by a different element outside of the normal Abwehr channels."

"Ah, so the Doctor may not be a German," said Tony.

Bill shook his head, "Well, MI5 thinks the Abwehr has gotten suspicious and have sent in a more hardened agent with a whole new operations and communication protocol."

"OK, then Bletchley needs a higher volume of intercepted messages from the Doctor to gain a mathematical advantage for cryptanalysis."

Bill nodded, "I suppose, you're the better expert on that one and to that end, MI5 gave me this telephone number for you to call as soon as you detect activity you suspect to be the Doctor. It's for the operations officer at the Morse intercept site at Knockholt, which is southeast of London." Bill referred to his notepad and read from it, "When you call, identify yourself as 'raconteur' and then state the five digits of the encoded frequency. They will repeat back the digits. Once you confirm their copy they will hang up. To encode the frequency, I'm reading verbatim now, use false subtraction to encode the frequency, using the last five digits of your service number as the minuend."

"Easy enough," said Tony.

"Glad that made sense to you. OK, MI5 is going to provide you with equipment to record suspected transmissions; I'll keep you posted on that," said Bill.

"Good, because the phone alert may not be fast enough for the intercept site to catch the high speed Morse transmissions. Once they make contact with control, they are done in say fifteen seconds, more or less, depending on the length of the message." said Tony.

"Alright Tony, that's what I have for you so far. I'll be bringing you back here for meetings with MI5 from time to time. They are a very competent and professional bunch, you'll like them."

**Wembley Park Flat
London**

Tony put his feet up on the edge of the small desk in his flat. He grinned at a small hole in the toe in one of his black GI socks, leaned back on the chair and slowly turned the frequency tuning knob on the modified radio. The circular frequency dial moved back and forth between the four and five megaHertz marks. It was 10:55 pm. The 'Doctor' had been observed using an 11:00 pm schedule to transmit on several occasions on the four-megaHertz frequency band; Tony hoped to catch him tonight, as he had on every night he was scanning. While sorting through the crackle of radio noise and myriad short wave transmissions in voice and Morse code in his headphones, his eyes moved around his upstairs flat. It was amply furnished and comfortable, although small. There were two rooms, one with a bath tub, toilet and wash basin. The other was his living, kitchen and bedroom with a single bed (one notch up from an army cot), a clothes chest, a small dining table, two straight-backed chairs and a comfortable stuffed chair. A single window by the table had a view to the street, when the blackout curtains weren't closed. His mind was thinking through all the information he knew about the Doctor while signals danced through his ears.

Tony's hand stopped instinctively when he heard a booming signal. It was a modulated continuous wave signal, same as that used by the Doctor. It was repeatedly calling one of the call signs that the Doctor had used in the past. It was him. He tuned for the center of the signal and interpolated the frequency from the markings on the dial. Tony quickly encoded the frequency and reported it to Knockholt. He then measured a DF line of bearing using the bezel mounted on the set. The Doctor's intended recipient acknowledged the Doctor's calls and within seconds the high speed transmission from the Doctor ripped across the airwaves and both sides of the contact went silent. He smiled and logged all the data into his observation journal. Finally, he got him after many hours had been spent, idly searching the high frequency bands. Hopefully, Knockholt had captured the signal and were now playing it back at normal speed and typing it onto an intercept message form. It would then be promptly couriered to Bletchley where the cryptanalysts would go to work on it. He couldn't wait for tomorrow morning. He got the map of London and the surrounding area out of his brief case and laid it out on the table. Tony mentally drew a line where his DF bearing on the Doctor would extend in both directions from his flat. The crude DF set did not have a means of determining from which direction the signal came. But, it was somewhere on the line centered on his flat, on the magnetic bearing he measured. He could hardly wait to plot his line with the lines from the U.K. direction finding sites so he could triangulate.

Captain Taylor and Tony spread an Army Air Force chart of London and suburbs onto the Captain's conference table. They came up with a compass and plotted the DF bearings reported from Bletchley's DF sites, including a British mobile van on the coast of the North Sea and of course the one taken from Tony's flat. "Damn," said Bill, "not a very tight cross of the bearings at all, that doesn't tell me much."

"Oh yes it does Bill, it tells you at the very least, what general area it's coming from. The best estimate is essentially the center of the triangular area these lines make. My guess is that area to the north of London is a good bet, albeit a big area. There's one line bearing that seems to be an outlier, but that's not unexpected, there will be outliers for numerous reasons."

Bill looked at Tony, "I think I understand what you just said," Tony started to reply but Bill continued, "just pulling your leg, go on."

"We've given MI5 some good info to chew on," said Tony. "As we overlay line bearings going forward, that area will tighten up. We'll get the Doctor, sooner or later."

"Keep at it Tony."

"Uh, Bill, just thinking, what's the chance we can get a mobile DF van to station itself where we can get a high quality cross bearing on that fix center, like here?" asked Tony pointing to a location on the map.

"None, the U.S. doesn't have any in the U.K.. I'm not sure if the Brits have any to spare but if they do, they've already thought of it or deployed one that's available, but, I'll ask."

"I have an idea. It looks like the evening hour frequencies he's used are consistently in the four to six megaHertz range. Ask the Brits for another short wave radio with a bandwidth filter for that specific frequency range. We'll put the wire recorder they're providing us on that radio's signal output. The Doctor's signal is so strong it will be the loudest thing on that band and I can turn on the recorder as soon as he opens his mouth. That will increase the probability that we'll get more of the encrypted messages he's sending. Meanwhile, I can also be getting a line bearing on him with the other radio. The decrypts of those messages are probably going to be a hell of a lot more valuable than his location anyway."

"Intriguing idea Tony." Captain Taylor picked up his phone and dialed. Tony listened as Bill related Tony's ideas. "That's great news, he's sitting in my office right now. Have a good afternoon." Bill's face now reflected a smile similar to the proverbial cat that ate the canary, "Well Tony, your idea will be implemented, but not by you. You've been cleared by Scotland Yard and are being reassigned back to Bletchley."

"I don't know whether to be happy or not, this has been fun," Tony said laughing, "but it certainly is good news."

"We'll keep your flat in London though and play all this by ear. But right now, it's more important that we get you back to Bletchley."

8 SOMETHING FISHY

A Block
Bletchley Park

"Good morning Commander," said Petra as he entered the office. "We were so relieved yesterday afternoon when we learned you were coming back."

"Thanks! I was too. It seemed like a bad dream to me. I'm so sorry for her family and friends."

Tony sat in the chair next to Petra's desk. A few awkward moments passed then Tony asked, "Any replacement for Molly?"

"Yes, a wren is coming over from Hut-6, Marion Kenny, she'll start next Monday," said Petra. "Meanwhile, I've been working long hours to keep up."

"Seems like it was just New Years. Time has sure flown by. When was the last time you were able to take a break, go home and see your parents?," said Tony.

"Right, I am planning a short visit home soon. Wednesday after next I'm taking the train. My father will pick me up at the station. I'll be back here Friday. I'm anxious to see my son. It's been a couple months."

"Will I have access while you're gone?" asked Tony.

She shrugged her shoulders, "Oh quite so, Marion will be fully briefed."

"What's your son's name? How old is he?" asked Tony.

She smiled, "Ives, after his great grandfather. He's nine but thinks he is 19—he's my treasure," she said proudly with slightly teary eyes. "Mum and dad are happy to be looking after him."

They hadn't spoken of their personal lives up to now. Tony wanted to pry further but decided not to push.

Tony got up, "I'm going down the hall to get some tea. Want me to bring you some?"

"Yes, please, thank you, plain," said Petra as she handed him her cup and saucer.

"I'll be careful with this," he said, admiring it. The sculptured surface that wrapped around the oversized cup had colorful flowers and green vines that cuddled a thatched roof cottage.

When he returned, Petra was in the process of putting files onto his work table. She looked up with a brief smile, "I took note of where you left off."

"I am not surprised," he said with a grin. She nodded with an appreciative smile.

"Tony, please pardon my melancholy. The reason they gave me some time off is because it will be a year since Harry, my late husband, an RAF pilot, was lost in a dog fight with German fighters off of France." She paused for a moment of reflection and went to work on a stack of paper in her basket.

He was pleased that she called him by first name. That was a first. "I'm so sorry Petra, I'm sure it's been difficult." Tony began reviewing the intercepted messages she gave him, "Really nice that your parents can take care of Ives. I have heard about people in London sending their children to places in the country, sort of like orphanages, until the war is over. Where do your folks live?"

"Near Ticknall, up north. They have a sheep farm, bloody good sized one too. It consumes my father's every waking moment. Can't convince him to slow down. I was born right there on the farm. It's a beautiful place with a proper stream running through it, a tributary of River Trent. I played there for hours when I was young."

"Any trout in it?"

She thought a bit, "I don't recall hearing about trout, but Harry caught bass, bream and perch. I don't think my father ever fished it. He thinks fishing is a waste of time better spent farming. Harry loved going down to catch breakfast at first light on weekends. His favorite breakfast was poached eggs, fish and fried tomatoes. He could eat fish every day and never tire of it. I'm not that fond."

Tony noticed her voice begin to falter a little with the reveries. "I love fly fishing especially for salmon, trout and bass. I grew up in a little town in Maine, Winter Harbor, right on the coast, in the northeast part of the state. Some of the best fishing in the world is in Maine, salt and fresh water alike, and oh such delicious lobsters!"

"I've never had lobster. What does your father do for a living?" she asked.

"Dad passed away last June. He had a machine shop in Ellsworth, a bigger town nearby, which my sister and I had no interest in running, so we sold it. Mom's been doing well, thanks partly to a very rewarding sale of that business and is leading a life of leisure and volunteering.

"Oh how bloody awful," she said, scanning his facial features intently as though for the first time, "I can't picture being without mum or dad, but it sounds as though she's getting on well."

He sighed, "Surprisingly well or a damn good facade. It was a very bad time for my sister and me. She is married so she could lean on her husband. I just dove in to my work. We all got through it in our own way. We think we have time to do things later. We just never know."

It seemed like a good place to stop talking and let bad memories fade to the background. It was refreshing to see Petra in a more personal light.

61

While Tony analyzed the files of decrypted German Navy messages, his mind also reviewed the possibilities and means of getting into the vault. Project Cigar seemed always to be in the background of his thoughts. He suspected that when Marion starts working in A Block, it would probably be more difficult to find an opportunity. "Well, that does it for this set of files Petra. Can you stop what you're doing to get another set? Or you can show me where these go and I'll get the next set myself."

She hesitated, looked at Tony for a moment, "Best I mind the rules Commander."

"I understand Petra, I wouldn't think of doing anything that would put you in jeopardy."

"Right." She took the files from Tony, returned them to the vault and brought out three more folders. "There, that should keep you occupied for a while. I'm going to get more tea, do you fancy some?" she asked. He nodded enthusiastically.

As soon as he heard the door shut, his mind clocked through the timing of going into the vault to figure out the filing system. The visualization of it all caused adrenalin to rush into his bloodstream. He took a deep calming breath when Petra came back into the office. There would not have been enough time for him to find and access the files he needed. He refocused on the texts of the decrypted and translated German Navy shore command, ship and submarine messages to and from their higher commands, including Berlin. His focus was centered on the decrypted messages from the high command short wave link between Berlin and Admiral Dönitz's U-boat force HQ in Lorient, France. He was gaining an insight of tremendous value. One that brought suspicion about the source of some of their intelligence.

A few days later, Tony studied several decrypted messages from Berlin to Admiral Dönitz that he had set aside today and over the past days. He was now convinced that the Germans had very probably broken the current U.S./U.K. maritime cypher or had acquired a spy in the U.S. or Britain with access to a lot of merchant marine operations information. The German intelligence on Allied merchant convoy operations was now too comprehensive and accurate to have been gleaned from open sources. Proving it would cause both governments to be embarrassed, since it had been only months since British Naval Cypher No. 2 was replaced for the same reason.

"Petra," Tony called out excitedly, "can we get Edwin to come over from Hut-6 to review some intel I found? Or if more convenient for him, I can go over there."

She picked up the phone and dialed, "Edwin, can you spare some time to meet with Commander Romella? Here or there, your choice. Jolly good!"

Petra hung up, "He'll be here in 15 minutes or so."

"Great, my conversations with him have really been enlightening. He really knows the German submarine problem well. I've found some things he'll find very interesting," said Tony.

"Thank you for your time Edwin," said Tony shaking Edwin's hand.

"Well now, me mate, what's my favorite Yank gotten into now?" replied Edwin grinning.

"Some bad news actually Edwin. When the Germans shifted to the new SHARK four-wheel Enigma and our decrypts dried up, I started paying close attention to the FISH decrypts, when we've been lucky enough to break into it. I've set aside several messages between Berlin and Admiral Dönitz that are very revealing. This one in particular is an intel summary of Allied merchant shipping convoy activity, sent from Berlin to Admiral Dönitz that's quite detailed and accurate. I just checked the plots of the convoys and they are spot on."

Edwin read the message carefully and cross-checked the info with the convoy chart that plotted reported positions and planned tracks. "Bloody hell. Extraordinary Tony."

"Yes, and about two hours later, Dönitz sent an urgent message to two wolfpacks. Traffic analysis of the message externals tells us that it's this wolfpack," Tony pointed to plots on the chart, "and Dönitz did that on an urgent basis because of a recent change in the track ordered by the U.S. Navy Commodore that's controlling that convoy," Tony pointed to convoy Y147's track on the chart.

"I can see how you can arrive at that conclusion Tony." Edwin digested the other decrypted messages Tony set aside. "None of these messages about convoys to Dönitz cite the source of their intelligence," said Edwin.

"Oh hell no, they are as smart as we are about sources of ULTRA intel. None of the Berlin intel summaries have ever revealed a source, at least none that I've seen. So, it's either HUMINT or Naval Cipher #3. I believe that the timeliness of the info they are providing Dönitz excludes HUMINT because of the time delays HUMINT reporting and processing would require."

Edwin and Tony spent the better part of a half hour pouring over all of Tony's analysis. "It's a very convincing conclusion Tony," said Edwin, "but still, it's going to be seen as circumstantial evidence up the line. We'll never get a definitive report out of here. This is a sticky wicket, yes? How did they break Cypher #3 so quickly?"

Tony sat quietly at his desk with his head down on crossed arms thinking intently about Edwin's rhetorical question and what to do about the evidence at hand. Several moments passed before he sat up grinning. "I have a plan!" He turned his attention back to the chart of the northeast Atlantic that had the latest wolfpack positions and patrol areas penciled, along with planned routes of merchant convoys headed to Britain.

"Do tell, what are you thinking" asked Edwin, watching anxiously.

"Petra, a message blank please?" asked Tony. "The message will speak for itself Edwin, give me a few minutes." Tony wrote a lengthy message to a select set of ULTRA intelligence addressees and handed it to Edwin. Petra read it over their shoulders.

"Bloody hell, Tony," said Edwin when he finished reading it, "that should jolly well do it. If I understand this, the Commodore of convoy Y147 will be sent message orders to change their route using Cypher #3. Then we watch to see if a wolfpack is redirected to a new intercept position reflecting that course change. Then we'll know they are bloody well reading Cypher #3. But, won't Y147 be put into jeopardy with this?"

Tony nodded, "Not really, they have been redirecting some U-boats from the North Atlantic to more southerly areas, as far south as Gibraltar. Y147 will be far enough out of range for those remaining up north that we can change their track back out of harm's way. We have a more secure channel we can use in this case, our destroyer escort communications." Edwin smiled, "Brilliant!"

Tony slapped Edwin's shoulder, "And DC can let us know when they transmit those orders to Y147 so we can start focusing on the FISH messages from Berlin to Dönitz as well as the U-boat communications broadcast from Dönitz to promptly catch their reaction. That's where you come in Edwin. Can you coordinate a focused effort of the FISH analysts and the intercept operators at the Knockholt intercept site on the U-boat broadcast once I know the deception message is sent to Y147?"

"I'll do what I can, ceteris paribus," said Edwin.

Tony smiled, "All things being equal, roger that. If we're not lucky enough to have a crib to decrypt the shortwave broadcast message from Dönitz that warns the U-boats about Y147, I'll at least be able to figure out that it's a response message from the urgency indicator and the addressees used previously when Dönitz responded to convoy intel."

Edwin nodded with an appreciative grin, "Right, we should be able to do this."

Tony nodded, "Understood. I'll be working the problem closely with DC also, so there's backup of sorts. Admiral Dönitz will be licking his chops to take that convoy out and will direct subs to intercept. The

Germans have not indicated that they are aware that we've added three tin cans, uh, destroyers, as a convoy protection force though. We've kept that out of the normal convoy communications channels. That sort of provides a counterbalance to laying bare the convoy's route. If a wolfpack closes in and sees those tins cans, they'll probably not chance an attack. They've been losing U-boats lately and communications between Berlin and Admiral Dönitz reflect great displeasure with some undue risks the U-boat captains have taken and the number of boats they've lost. I'm sure Dönitz has made that clear to the U-boat captains. At any rate, if the Germans respond fairly quickly, we'll know it's not a HUMINT source. As soon as I get the info on the deception message transmission, I'll give you a shout." Edwin nodded.

"But Tony," Petra interrupted, "You realize that you'll need to get all this transmitted through your own channels, it can't leave from Bletchley, for a number of reasons."

"Mainly Hardcastle, I know," said Tony. "I'll handle it. A quick trip to London is in order. I hope you two don't tattle on me." He said it rather kiddingly, but he wasn't kidding. Either one of them could whisper to Hardcastle and he would be in an uncomfortable situation.

She shook her head smiling, "Tickety-boo."

Edwin nodded in agreement, "Quite!"

9 THE DOCTOR'S IN A FIX

U.S. Naval Attaché Office
London

"Good afternoon Captain," said Tony as he entered Captain Taylor's office. "Lieutenant Jacob told me that you delayed your departure for MOD earlier to sign the release for my message. I really appreciate that. I wanted it on Commander Safford's desk in the morning. He'll have a lot of coordinating and selling to do over there in Main Navy and time is of the essence."

"No thanks are necessary, Tony, do you have anything else for me? There's a little happy hour thing coming up in two hours at the Russian Embassy that I don't want to miss, but I have a little time."

Tony laughed, "Better you than me on that one. I do have a couple things I wanted to pass on sir. Marion Kenny, an enlisted wren, started her assignment in the archive today. She's a permanent replacement for Molly, transferred from Hut-6, where they work the German Navy problem. I met her before I left, but didn't have much time to spend chatting."

Captain Taylor acknowledged, "Have a seat Tony. Interesting and quite obvious why they put an enlisted in there. Hardcastle's good, she won't be on your list of officer equivalents. What's your impression of Marion?"

"I know what you're asking. All in all, I think she'll toe the line and follow the rules," said Tony. "I don't think that her being there will make it easier for me to get access to any Cigar stuff."

"OK. Uh, how long do you think it will be 'til you see a response to the convoy deception message?" asked Bill.

"It will take a day or so for Commander Safford to get it coordinated, approved and transmitted. We'll focus on pertinent decrypts after the message is transmitted to the convoy but it will be a day or so for the Germans to decrypt it and react. I'll keep you posted."

"Good. Oh, by the way, did you see that General MacArthur and his family was evacuated from Corregidor by PT boat? They made it to Mindanao OK."

"Oh, good, the last I heard was that he was being evacuated by submarine. I'm glad OP-20G ordered the evacuation of our people out of that tunnel too. I sure they all made it out OK, I haven't seen anything on that. Oh, before I forget it Bill, you asked me to let you know if I saw any indication of the Germans being aware of the British Operation Chariot. I have seen nothing about Chariot in any of the Berlin decrypts that they have any awareness of the operation. It might help my analysis if you can you tell me more about it in case they aren't using the operation's nickname."

Bill nodded, "Now that it's getting close to its D-day, currently 28 March, I can give you some Top Secret info, well, their Most Secret info, so you can keep a sharper eye for anything concerning it. It's going to be a very large amphibious commando raid on the lock gates of the Normandie dry dock at Saint-Nazaire. At D-2, afloat units will sail from Falmouth."

"Aha," exclaimed Tony as the light bulb came on, "I wondered for a moment why that dry dock, then I got it. The Germans would be hard pressed to deploy the Battleship Tirpitz from Norway into the North Atlantic without that dry dock's availability. And the Tirpitz could, at the very least, raise holy hell with our shipping to Britain. So keeping her away is strategically sound."

"Exactly Tony, that's the largest dry dock in the world and the Tirpitz needs that facility, or she'll have to go all the way back to German ports and she'll be vulnerable getting there, especially from the Atlantic. So, this is a critically important raid. It's a heavily guarded area and surprise will be absolutely critical."

"Understood Bill, I'll be alert for indications that it's compromised. Good grief, the shit will sure hit the German fan when that comes off."

"Alright Tony, do you have anything else?"

"Well," responded Tony taking a breath, "Petra will be taking some time off to go north and visit with her mother and father. I'll have a few days in the archive with Marion. I'll be alert for a low risk opportunity to get into that vault."

"Be real careful Tony. In fact, make sure the conditions are such that you won't get caught. Given all that's transpired, it would probably be better to wait for a level of trust to develop that will result in them allowing you to go in there."

"Aye, aye sir. I'm not sure that level of trust will ever be achieved, it's just pure office procedures, policies and politics. I'll be cautious."

"I'll update Winant so he won't think we're coasting. He asked me about it after yesterday's senior embassy staff meeting."

"And boss, I have been thinking. A miniature camera would be good to have, you know like the pocket sized ones we had on that Moscow trip. I could record documents quickly, without removing them. As it is, if I do find something, I'll have to find a way to get them to the cottage, photograph them and then get them back. That's just going to be too risky," said Tony.

Bill paused a moment, "I'll try and get one for you. No, I'm sure I can get my hands on one. What's the latest on you and the Doctor?"

Tony grinned, "The wideband receiver, wire recorder and DF set are at my Bletchley cottage and it's all working just fine. I heard the Doctor last night and the night before." He reached into his left jacket pocket and pulled out an envelope. "Here are the DF bearings on each of those transmissions and the wire reels from the recorder. The Brit's COMINT and DF site at Knockholt should have had sufficient time to intercept the transmissions too."

"Bravo zulu! I'll call over to MI5 and follow up," said Bill.

Tony unrolled the chart they used previously to plot the Doctor's bearings, spread it out on the conference table, put desk items on the four corners and plotted Tony's new line bearings. Bill took notes during his phone call with MI5 then returned to the table,

"MI5 also got DF bearings on each of those transmissions and were happy to get your info. They shared their DF data with me and said they are getting a mobile DF van assigned to this case. It will be operational tomorrow morning." Tony added the plots of the line bearings from the British DF sites. They stood looking at the results of all the lines running across the chart, each labeled with date, time and intercept site.

"Damn it's getting confusing now," said Tony, "just enough data to be intriguing, not enough to be conclusive." Tony studied the plots intently. "Bill, these are ground wave signals measured by their sites and me and I put a lot of validity to them. It's my contention at this point that the transmitter was not at the same location in every instance it transmitted." Tony noted the surprise on Bill's face, "You heard me right. The transmitter is either mobile or there are two of them. Look, here's one set of cross bearings and here's another. Taken separately, they make two comparatively good fixes. One is up here outside London, out by Lady Watson's general area actually. The other is way the hell out in the Milton-Keynes area."

Bill looked up from the chart, "You told me you could tell unique qualities about a transmitter by ear, what's your take on what you heard?"

"Given what is best described as fist characteristics in the manual Morse callups and the sound of the signal itself, it's always the same operator. So, it's the same or a same model transmitter equipment that is being used at two locations."

Bill thought for a few moments, "Why would the same agent transmit from different locations?"

"I would say most likely for purposes of foiling our direction finding efforts, security situations at their mansion, or expediency."

"Does this revelation give you any more ideas?" asked Bill.

"Let's do two things. One, keep plotting the bearings to find out if there seems to be consistency in this two location theory. Hopefully, the British mobile van will be a big help resolving the ambiguities in the fix areas by contributing geometrically significant cross bearings." Bill acknowledged. Tony continued, "And secondly, find a way to get me the use of an unmarked car for a couple days so I can recon these fix areas to see if anything stimulates my imagination or kicks curiosity into gear as I drive around those areas. I'd take my jeep, but that would damn sure stick out like a sore thumb."

"You better forget the car recon idea. That MI5's domain. I'll share your mobile transmitter and two fix theory with MI5 though," said Bill. "By the way Tony, you and I are going to Havenwood Saturday. Lady Watson invited us both for tea, dinner and breakfast. You didn't have anything planned did you?" he asked with a grin.

"I don't get the feeling that it matters," said Tony with a chuckle.

Bill smiled, "Well, I would convey your regrets if you had something more important, really. So barring that, get back down here Friday afternoon so we can review the week and then go have a pint."

"You realize boss, I can't listen for the Doctor or study decrypts if I'm at Havenwood!"

"Yes, but MI5 will have the mobile van operating and in the final analysis, it is MI5's spy problem to solve and they have good resources on it now; the decrypts will be waiting patiently for you."

"But Bill…"

"No buts Tony, you're going and don't forget to bring an overnight bag. I need your connection with the good Russian Major to do some probing. He never paid as much attention to me. There's quite a controversy about us sharing intel on German troop movements with Moscow, even though they are quote an ally unquote. We gave them some intel we learned from decrypts that we could plausibly mask as coming from a human source so we don't divulge that we're reading high level German Army communications. Basically it drew the conclusion that Hitler was marshalling forces to the east to attack Russia. It was taken as ridiculous info by the Russian high command. They are just as dubious about sharing intel with us and are giving us crap we already know. Be alert for any hints about intel sources and sharing Kiminko might have."

Havenwood Estate
Suburb of London

Formal tea in Lady Watson's dining room was again splendid. Each of His Majesty's armed services was represented. So too was the egotistical and ever inquisitive Russian Major Kiminko and his less than gregarious bride. Their places were across from Tony and Bill. All but one of the 16 place settings on the brilliant white table cloth were claimed by the guests, standing tall, relatively quiet behind their chairs in their dress uniforms and afternoon dresses, awaiting Lady Watson. Tony spent the idle time admiring the furnishings. The medieval table and high backed chairs drew one's eye to their sculptured ornamentations. The tea cups and saucers were thin and opaque but beautifully decorated with the Watson crest and artful trimmings. A soft applause filled the room when Lady Watson swept into the room in her pastel blue and green silk dress. She went straight to her chair, a light rouge blush on her cheeks and nodded for everyone to take their seats. "Please ladies and gentleman, do relax and good afternoon to you all." Everyone greeted her in return. Inga's staff immediately began bringing tea and finger sandwiches on silver trays from grand Louis XIV side tables.

Major Kiminko resumed the conversation with Bill and Tony that he started in the library while waiting for the call to the table. "Commander Romella, what is the most interesting thing you've learned in England so far?"

"The beauty of the white cliffs of Dover, Major, without a doubt," said Tony, even though he had not in fact seen them yet. Bill and Tony suffered through several other topics and questions, ranging from small talk to issues involving German military activities. They countered the Major at every turn when he probed sensitive areas. All the while the Major's wife sat quiet but attentive.

Bill and Tony did learn one significant piece of information that they would report to Washington. The Russians have heard that President Roosevelt had plans to round up Japanese citizens residing in the United States and inter them in camps for the duration of the war with Japan.

As the closing hour on the tea soirée was approaching, guests began moving toward the door, taking their leave.

"You both are staying for dinner and breakfast, of course," Lady Inga whispered to Bill and Tony.

"At your pleasure Inga," said Bill.

"Most certainly, everyone else has plans of their own, so it will be just us, informal and relaxing," she said, smiling. "You two are a long way from home without your families and I would like to rescue you from your troubles and rigors."

"A pleasure and an honor Inga, although we know little of boredom," said Bill.

Tony nodded in agreement, "It's a beautiful estate with many sights for sore eyes. You're a gracious host and I appreciate being here."

"I am pleased you are enjoying yourselves, now I must go and visit with the Thornhills up the lane a bit. They are hosting a reception for some neighbors and friends and I must pay my respects. You two make yourselves at home. I'll see you in the library before dinner."

"My respects to Gwyn," said Tony.

"Oh my, do we fancy her now?" Inga asked with a raised eyebrow and smile.

"No, no Inga, nothing like that, she was fun on the dance floor, but too young for me," said Tony blushing.

Inga laughed, "The single ladies of vintage over the whole of England shall breathe a sigh of relief tonight that their hopes are not dashed." They all laughed.

Tony and Bill went to the library to relax and wait for Inga's return. They sat in large deeply stuffed leather arm chairs on either side of a medieval period side table with a stunning antique lamp. Bill pulled a cigar and match box from his inside jacket pocket and struck a match on the emery coated side of the box. He puffed a few times until the end glowed bright orange. The smoke billowed upward toward the high ceiling. "Major Kiminko and his wife are both interesting and puzzling aren't they Tony?"

"Yes, I always have the feeling something is stirring deep inside them," said Tony.

Bill chuckled and puffed a smoke ring over the top of the lamp so it would catch the light emanating from the circular opening in the top, "Yes, I agree, he tends to raise a caution flag with his line of questioning at times. Everyone understands that attachés have but one primary purpose, to gather intelligence and useful information. But the good Major is clearly two clicks past that."

"One thing I noticed Bill, he's particularly interested in naval information. But that could be just with you and me. And by the way, a couple things he said, today and previously, have led me to believe that he knows you and I spent some time in Moscow."

"Oh really?" asked Bill as he turned his gaze to the light shade, "Exquisite piece. As for Moscow, I've never told him nor have we discussed it before."

"Well, he knows about it," said Tony, "for whatever it's worth."

Bill snuffed his cigar in a white and black marble ash tray on the table, laid his head back and closed his eyes. Tony got up and scanned the wall library shelves for the Cambridge documents about the miniature

Stonehenge. All four walls had built-in libraries six shelves high. One wall appeared to be for medieval period volumes. Half way around the room, he found a shelf with several soft-covered documents. One was a Cambridge tome with a soft spine hand labeled "Diminutive Stonehenge." It included several folded architectural drawings and illustrations along with many pages of double spaced typewritten information. He removed it from the shelf and took it to a table in the center of the library. He was barely aware of Bill's muffled snoring and totally unaware of the passage of time as he soaked up Cambridge's comprehensive study on the site.

"I see you have found the lot of it," said Inga as she entered the library. "Is the Captain feeling poorly?"

Her voice caused Tony to turned with a start, "He's fine, just napping. How are the Thornhills?"

"Quite fine sir, and Gwyn asked me to offer her respects, I think she fancies you Tony," said Inga with a devilish grin, "she asked why I didn't bring you."

Bill piped up, "All the ladies like him, he's young, handsome and has money."

She laughed, "Do they now? Well, he puts on a darling performance as a confident, reserved man with great self-control," teased Inga, pausing to watch Tony's face turn red.

"It's dark already, I need to go topside, take a short nap and freshen up," said Tony, changing the line of conversation.

"When shall we knock you up?" asked Inga. "Don't fuss much, it's an informal dinner, casual."

"Oh, in that case, a half hour before the dinner bell would be fine, thank you," said Tony.

"Same for me," added Bill.

They feasted on a hearty lamb stew, dark bread and cheese, followed by a rich vanilla pudding. They retired to a sitting room for port and conversation about all manner of things until after midnight. The lower the level in the crystal decanter became, the happier and giddier the conversations became. "Oh gentleman, I can't tell you how long it's been that I've enjoyed myself so much," said Inga.

Bill arose from the deep chair, after one unsuccessful try, "I better hit the rack or I'll never make it onto a horse in the morning."

"Me too," Tony said laughing, "this stuff sneaks up on you."

"If you both insist, I'll have to do the same," said Inga laughing like a school girl.

They chatted and joked as they walked up the staircase to the second floor. Bill's room was first down the hallway, then Tony's and at the end was Inga's suite.

"Thank you and good night Inga, it was a wonderful diversion," said Tony as he came to his door.

"Give us a hug," said Inga, "I had a bloody wonderful a time." He attempted to give a gentlemanly hug, but Inga pulled him close. "You must come to visit more often Tony," she said softly and kissed his cheek.

"You will just have to invite me more often." Their eyes locked for a moment, he leaned hesitantly toward her and kissed her cheek briefly. He felt his face turn hot, "I'm sorry Inga, this damn sherry has made me stupid."

She grinned at him, "Not at all, and I shall." With that, she turned away and headed down the hallway toward her suite. He watched her for a few moments before entering his room.

Tony and Bill were riding at Inga's sides toward the woods. "You're riding like an old ranch hand Bill," Tony called over past Inga.

"I never laid a hand on a horse until Inga coerced me into giving it a try," Bill replied.

"Have you been to the little Stonehenge?" asked Tony.

"No, that should be interesting," said Bill.

"And so you shall," Inga said and kicked her horse gently into a gallop. Tony and Bill followed her into the woods. They rode a winding narrow foot path that seemed at times like a never ending path through a huge maze in a fantasy. "Mind your heads," she called out now and then to warn them of low hanging branches.

The ten minute chase brought them to the stream and small clearing adjacent to the hidden circle of stones. They dismounted, tied their horses to branches and walked through the brush to the site of bygone era remnants. "Amazing," was all Bill could say. The same magic overtook him over as it did Tony. Inga sat patiently on what Tony imagined to be a former altar of sorts in the center of the array of stones. Bill and Tony wandered among the stones independently, touching and examining each one.

Tony stopped short with an inquisitive, concentrating look on his face. "What is it?" asked Bill.

"I swear I just heard Morse code," said Tony. In a short time, very faint Morse code sounds found their way to all their ears. Each nodded acknowledgement. Tony strained to hear it well enough to read it.

When the Morse stopped Bill asked, "Could you make out what it said?"

"No, it was too weak, probably coming from a window that's ajar," he said convincingly although it was a lie. "Inga, what's over in that direction?" Tony pointed at the woods in the direction the Morse was coming from.

"You don't know?" she asked, "The Russian Embassy rented that small estate just the other side of my fence. Major Kiminko, his wife and a small staff live there."

Tony and Bill looked at each other. The look of total surprise was splashed all over their faces. "What is it?" she asked.

Bill shrugged, "Nothing, except that we had no idea where he lived and I certainly didn't expect to find diplomatic residences out here. It's rather remote from the rest of the Russian Embassy facilities."

She laughed, "It's no palace, it was a quite run down manor that had been vacant several years. The daughter of the owners hoped to occupy it after the war, but as things got lean, she was forced to put it up for let, hoping to sell it, poor dear. The Major told me that his wife feared the German bombs in London proper, so that answers for renting out here."

U.S. Naval Attaché Office
London

Bill called Tony to his office when the Monday morning classified pouches arrived by British courier. They gave their attention first to the pouch from MI5. The report on radio activities of the Doctor contained several new intercepts, each with a direction finding fix. Tony plotted the fixes on the chart they were keeping on the Doctor. "Bill, look at the date and time of this fix," said Tony pointing to the dot representing the center of a fix area.

Bill read the data detail of the intercept and looked up at Tony, "The fix area encompasses Kiminko's estate! And it's the same time we heard the Morse code, I took particular note of the time I heard it."

Tony smiled, "Yes, so did I and those are the call signs I heard coming from that estate. The Doctor is a member of the Russian Embassy staff, perhaps the Major or his wife. I'll put 20 bucks on the Major."

Bill laughed, "I'm not going against that bet. But that would make him a traitor if he's communicating with the Germans and I can't picture him in that role. Not the scornful way he talks about the Germans. If it is him, he's a hell of a good actor."

"Or there's a Russian double agent coordinator in Western France that the Doctor is communicating with rather than the Germans. How much more interesting can this get?" asked Tony with a grin. My question now is, where's that second location and why does the Doctor need to use it?"

"That reminds me Tony, I got a call from MI5. They did some recon on that second fix area. They have a building in that area that they were curious about and learned that it was rented by someone on their watch list. They have kept an eye on the place and determined that this person has had contact with the Kiminkos at that building, no less. They saw the Kiminkos arrive there on foot in work clothes one evening and stay for 38 minutes and return to their sedan a couple blocks away. MI5 has no idea what's going on there. It's an old garage of sorts. They're puzzled but are thinking, given some other intel they have, that there's probably explosives in there. All windows are painted black and there seems to be someone there at all times. MI5 will get it figured out."

10 SETTING THE TRAP

The Mansion
Bletchley Park

Tony immediately threw himself into analyzing the German submarine force related decrypts upon returning to Bletchley. It only took three days before the evidence was clear – the Germans took the bait. Berlin advised Admiral Dönitz of the new track of the convoy but warned of the potential danger presented by U.S. Navy destroyers that might be escorting the convoy. Dönitz immediately sent two wolfpacks urgent advisories. Tony sat back and took a deep breath. Hardcastle had decreed that no reports would be submitted by Tony out of Bletchley Park without passing them through him first. At the same time, it was absolutely imperative that he promptly report this information somehow to Captain Taylor, the OPCEN and OP-20G. From a political perspective, telling Hardcastle about the mechanism used to confirm the evidence and Tony's role in it would start a bonfire. Secondly, there would be a delaying factor since Hardcastle would have the analysts study this to death and given their workload, there would be no telling how long that might take. Even then, there would be no guarantee Bletchley would report it as promptly as Tony felt prudent given the embarrassment of Cypher #3's compromise. He decided to try and work the politics first and use the end run as a backup approach. He began putting together his presentation to Hardcastle.

Tony waited patiently at his desk in the loft of the mansion garage. Two cups of tea later, he saw Hardcastle's yeoman at the top of the loft stairs motioning, "Captain Hardcastle will see you now sir."

Tony gave her a thumb up, "Thank you petty officer, I'll be right there." He picked up his file folders, and mentally reviewed his approach as he walked to Hardcastle's office.

"Good morning Captain. I've worked diligently to confirm a discovery and as you directed, I want to brief you prior to reporting the information through both of our channels."

"Right, go on," Hardcastle replied through a poker face and motioned for Tony to sit in the chair alongside the Captain's desk.

Tony sat down and gathered in a full breath. "I'll summarize first, then go back through the details. B-Dienst analysts in Berlin have broken the current merchant marine cypher, which is being used by the U.S., Canada and the U.K. for encrypting classified messages to and from North Atlantic convoys transiting to and from U.K. ports…"

Hardcastle interrupted, "No, no, that's old information, they broke Cypher number two last September and we changed to Cypher three promptly. That's only a few months past, you're looking at old information." To say that Tony had scratched an open wound would be an understatement.

"Begging the Captain's pardon sir, I'm aware of the compromise of number two. This sir, is clearly an exploitation of number three given the dates of the message intercepts and decrypts," said Tony.

Hardcastle crossed his arms on his chest so tightly that his black uniform tie buckled up, "I'll believe it when I see it. You said you had details. Just get on with it Commander, but I'll bloody well have naval analysts research it."

Tony opened the cumbersome fat file on his lap and placed a copy of a message in front of the Captain. "This sir, is a message sent last Tuesday from the staff of Admiral Morton, who commands our Merchant Marine, to the Commodore of convoy Y147. They gave the Commodore a revised track to take the convoy on a more northerly path. That was done because there was ULTRA intelligence indicating a German wolfpack was being vectored by Admiral Dönitz's staff to intercept them about 200 nautical miles west of the U.K.. That convoy is carrying among other things, aviation fuel, aircraft engines and classified shipborne air search radar systems. Our Chief of Naval Operations thought the risk of hinting we had information on their wolfpack location was reasonable, given the high value of the convoy and OK'd rerouting Y147. Also, the convoy has three tin cans for an escort." Tony paused for Hardcastle to scan the message. "Now then, 58 hours after that message was transmitted on the shortwave broadcast to the convoy, and note, encrypted with Cypher three," Tony then handed the Captain the decrypted message, "This message is from Berlin to Admiral Dönitz advising him of Y147's new track and warned of possible destroyer escorts. This is an obvious prompt response to decrypting our Cypher three message to the convoy. Then, sir, Dönitz sent this urgent message to the wolfpack flotilla commanders tasked to that ocean zone, probably vectoring them to an intercept point on convoy Y147's new track, and I might add, probably warned them of the danger from combatant escorts." Tony paused as the Captain read.

"This last message isn't a decrypt and we have no idea what's in it? Asked Hardcastle pointedly. "Perhaps it's just a coincidence Commander, yes?"

"Perhaps sir, but if I may, Berlin's decrypt clearly reflects the contents of the Cypher three encrypted message. And, I have two other incidents that occurred in the last ten days where wolfpack vectoring took place shortly after orders of changes in convoy routing were sent. I have the info with me if you'd care to review…"

"Never mind, Lieutenant Commander. This all seems, uh, inconclusive. They have a very effective intelligence system," Hardcastle barked. Tony was fighting hard to hold back his response as the Captain stared daggers. "You will not, I repeat not, report these observations. Our analysts will review your documents. Leave them with me, and if they feel it warrants reporting, they will make proper reports. And, I have the distinct feeling that you violated our agreement concerning your activities here…"

"Sir, I did not submit a report without clearing it with you. I did make an operational suggestion to DC, which was accepted and acted upon by others."

Hardcastle was fuming, "Can't you see what an embarrassing false alarm this could possibly be for our governments? We have to fight hard for the resources to do our job here and turmoil like this might bring attention we don't need. Do not report a word of this."

Tony was disappointed at Hardcastle's response, but not surprised, "Sir, with all due respect, I have discussed this with the navy analysts in A Block and they concur with my findings. I am briefing you as a courtesy. It is my duty to report to U.S. officials the results of the work I have performed."

"Like bloody hell you will!" yelled Hardcastle, "Heed my warning Commander. Do not report this."

"By your leave sir?" asked Tony perfunctorily, already rising and starting for the door. Hardcastle responded with a string of mumbles that Tony didn't even attempt to hear.

U.S. Naval Attaché Office
London

Tony knocked on Captain Taylor's office door and entered, "Captain, I drove down to report news about that convoy Y147 message. The short story is that U.K. Cypher number three has been broken by the Germans. Dönitz vectored a wolfpack in response. Good news is, they also suspect tin cans in company so they probably cautioned the wolfpack accordingly."

"Have a seat Tony," said Captain Taylor.

"I must tell you sir that I tried to run it through Hardcastle a couple hours ago, but he was livid and ordered me not to report it. I couldn't bring copies of the evidence, of course, but I can sit down and write a very detailed report from memory. It will be enough for Washington to get started on the problem in the meantime."

"OK Tony, do it," said Bill.

"Also sir, along with reporting the compromise of Cypher three, we need to try and get Admiral Morton appraised via a special channel so he can make sure he's aware of the compromise and that he's aware that wolfpacks have been vectored."

"I have a meeting at the Admiralty to attend right now; use my office, get it all down on paper, draft the messages we need and we'll talk about it all when I get back. I'll give the Admiralty a heads up and work the politics so Hardcastle won't eat you alive. Don't leave this office or talk with anyone in the meantime. You better plan to stay in London tonight."

11 OH HALE

Wembley Park Flat
London

Tony awoke startled from loud knocking on the door. "Who is it?" he yelled out, having finally cleared away the cobwebs of deep sleep.

"Inspector Hale, Scotland Yard." Tony's heart skipped a beat. He remembered the gut wrenching feelings he experienced the last time he spoke with the Inspector.

"Coming," yelled Tony, as he searched with his feet for slippers. Having Hale on his doorstep was puzzling; Tony had been cleared. The cold wooden floor sent chills into his bare feet which slid quickly into his slippers, finding warmth in the rabbit fur lining. He grabbed a robe from the foot of the bed. He glanced at the window; it was still dark out since there was no hint at all of light around the edges of the blackout curtain. He fumbled with the lock on the door and opened it. "Please come in Inspector," said Tony as he twisted the round switch on the wall by the door and brought light to the room after the door shut.

Inspector Hale came in with a uniformed officer behind him. The Inspector looked around the flat briefly while the officer stood rigid at the door. "What is it Inspector?"

"I'll get right to it," Hale said, his eyes burning into Tony's as he spoke. His look sent alarm racing through Tony's mind. Just then Hale spotted the short wave radio on the desk. "Rather odd looking radio Commander."

"Inspector, I borrowed that from the Naval Attaché office to maintain my competency in Morse code. I'm a short wave enthusiast, a ham operator. One must constantly practice to maintain speed and accuracy."

"Indeed," said Hale. "I should be able to confirm that with the embassy, should I not?"

"Absolutely Inspector. Captain William Taylor, U.S. Naval Attaché can confirm that for you sir."

Hale scribbled briefly onto a hand memo book, took a seat at the small dinner table by the window, motioned for Tony to do the same. "Commander, starting with your departure from Captain Hardcastle's office yesterday morning, tell me where you've been."

"Ah, so Hardcastle put you up to this with some cock and bull story," said Tony, "That man is the most vengeful officer I know. He'll stop at nothing.."

Hale interrupted, "Save the tommyrot for another bloke Lieutenant Commander."

Tony grabbed a pencil that was lying on the table and began tapping the eraser end to drain energy and regain his composure. "OK Inspector, I went directly from Captain Hardcastle's office to the communications center where I drafted a message to my operational commander, Captain Taylor at our embassy advising that I'd be returning. I then went directly to the archive at A Block and returned a file I used to brief Captain Hardcastle. I then went to the canteen for tea and a sandwich. After that, I went to the motor pool for my jeep, returned to London and went directly to our embassy. I left the embassy about 4pm. I took the tube from the embassy, walked to a pub for a pint and a shepherd's pie. I came here, read the newspaper, went to bed and awoke when you knocked."

Inspector Hale said nothing but took notes during Tony's accounting of his time. Hale looked up at Tony, "Did you sit with or otherwise speak with anyone at the canteen?"

"No, there were only a few people I knew there, none of them very well and I sat alone," said Tony."

"Were you with Second Officer Moira O'Riordan at any time after you took tea at the canteen?" asked Hale.

"No, we've talked in the canteen a few times about playing a part in a skit, but only briefly. It's been probably a week or more since the last time."

Hale paused in deep thought, "Directly from the canteen to the motor pool?"

"Yes sir."

"Alone?"

"Yes, alone," said Tony, his irritation now obvious.

"Tell me more about your relationship with Second Officer O'Riordan," said Hale.

"Relationship? There is no relationship, we've only talked in the canteen. I recall that she joined Molly and me for dinner at the pub on one occasion but that's been quite a month or more ago. That's it."

"Has she been to your cottage? Or this flat?" asked Hale.

"Neither. Never. Why are you focusing so intently on her Inspector?" Tony was now fearing the worst, another victim.

Hale ignored Tony's question and continued, "You did not see her in any capacity in the past 48 hours?"

"Absolutely not." Tony was beginning to get a sick feeling about this line of questioning.

Hale looked up from his notes, "I am sorry Lieutenant Commander, but I must advise you not to leave London pending further investigation into the murder of Second Officer Moira O'Riordan. Captain Taylor will be informed."

Tony could feel the blood drain from his face, leaving him dizzy. He folded his arms on the table, "Oh my God," he whispered. "Where? How?" he asked.

"I cannot provide any details at the moment Commander," said Hale on his way out the door.

12 A HAVENWOOD AFFAIR

U.S. Naval Attaché Office
London

Captain Taylor shook Tony's hand vigorously then shut his office door. "Good God Tony, you sure manage to stir the pot. Have a seat. It might have been a bad night, but I have two sets of good news."

"I could use just one," said Tony.

"Scotland Yard has already dropped you as a suspect in O'Riordan's murder, abruptly, without explanation. I've spoken with MI5 and they had no meaningful comment about this event. But, I got the feeling that the Yard dropped you due to input from MI5. And seriously, MI5 is on general quarters with this murder. Something is utterly amiss. These murders have a very high level of pressure coming down on MI5. It's obvious to me that, given some hints from MI5 and MOD recently, they are suspecting covert operatives in these murders."

Tony took a deep sigh of relief, "And I'm getting hopping pissed off with Scotland Yard knocking at my door about it all and I damn sure won't miss them. The second good news item?"

The Captain filled a hand carved pipe in the shape of a destroyer's bow and lit it as he spoke, halting for puffs, "Washington and the Royal Navy both congratulated us on your report about the compromised convoy cyphers. They are in the process of coordinating the emergency implementation of a reengineered system that has vastly improved security design. They are passing interim instructions and procedures to all Commodores at sea through other channels until all the ships underway have had a chance to get the new machines. These interim procedures, basically double encryption, are probably not going to hold up long against B-Dienst either, but they will definitely buy time."

"Thanks Bill. The convoy track information is perishable, so by the time they break through the double encryption, the intel may be useless. But if someone is providing them the new crypto equipment design and daily settings," he paused, "well, I don't even want to think that. I'm sure Washington and London will work that out."

Bill got a smile on his face, "Oh and you'll love this, when certain people at the Admiralty found out about Hardcastle's hamstringing, they found a way to politely advise him that it was inappropriate for security reasons and beyond his authority."

"Praise the Lord," said Tony laughing, "but I know he won't take that lightly. He'll find some way to make me pay." They both laughed.

Bill's phone rang. Tony watched as Bill jotted notes. "OK Mike, I'll tell Tony. He'll appreciate hearing this."

"What will I appreciate?" asked Tony when Bill hung up.

"That was Mike Nelson, an intelligence agent posted here at the embassy as a Trade Representative. He's from Roosevelt's Office of the Coordination of Information. Mike's working directly for the Director, General William Donovan. Those facts and what I'm about to tell you is Top Secret. Mike's been working closely with MI5 and MI6. He just told me that Washington decrypted the messages to and from the Doctor that shed a lot of light. The information was shared with MI5 but it didn't seem to be much of a surprise, so they probably decrypted them too, they just kept it close to the chest. I'll skip all the details but the Doctor is in fact a German agent. His mission appears to be related to gaining communications and crypto systems information from Bletchley Park and there's some other mission that's unclear at this time. The Doctor reported terminating Molly and Moira due to being uncooperative and therefore a risk. MI5 says that if the Doctor is not successful in getting someone to give him information, he has no choice but to kill them to preserve the identity and mission of all involved."

"As the Brits would say, bloody awful," said Tony. "I shudder to think that Molly's relationship with me was something the Doctor thought would be a sufficient vulnerability to support blackmail. She wasn't married though, so that doesn't really make sense."

Bill rubbed his chin, "But it's common knowledge that Captain Hardcastle put out the word that females at Bletchley were not to date any Americans. Ridiculous as that policy sounds, he could conceivably ruin someone's career over it or at the very least, make their life miserable."

"I'll never date another British woman," said Tony.

"Your nose is growing longer Tony," said Bill with a chuckle.

Tony smiled, "OK boss, why did Mike authorize you to share this with me?"

Bill sat back in his chair and thought for a brief moment, "Hardcastle refuses to budge about bringing you back into Bletchley until he meets with the MOD. Ambassador Winant was briefed and told me he would work on the issue. So, that leaves you here at the embassy until the politics get resolved. Unfortunately, MI5 cannot normally share classified information with Scotland Yard or in this case, even Hardcastle."

"Damn! There's some things at the cottage I need to get if I'm going to be here a while," said Tony.

"You can go back to the cottage and get what you need. Just don't go into Bletchley," said Bill.

"OK, where do we go from here?"

A subtle grin formed on Bill's face, "We get the Doctor!" Tony chuckled. Bill looked Tony square in the eye and said, "I'm dead serious. We're up to our necks with the Brits to get that bastard! Dead or alive. It's a really, really hot item."

Tony thought for a moment then looked at Bill with a quizzical look, "Where in hell do I come in on that?"

"You already started with the radio intercepts and direction finding. Look Tony, your instincts are excellent, just use them to best advantage. Tomorrow afternoon Mike and MI5 will be here to meet with us. This is a high priority for both governments because with just one success, the Doctor could compromise Bletchley and that would be an astounding loss. To give you a feel for the level of interest in this, Churchill and Roosevelt have been briefed and agreed to have our intelligence services cooperate fully. Anything you need, anything at all, just tell me and we can probably get it for you. I've already asked for a personal weapon for you."

Tony got up and paced, "Oh boy, I'm in deep shit now huh boss?" He couldn't help but laugh.

Bill laughed, "The meeting tomorrow with MI5 will set up a mechanism of coordination so we don't waste time and resources. By the way, there is something else I need to share with you that I was not at liberty to share before. Lady Watson is cooperating closely with my office and MI5, sharing whatever tidbits she picks up from her foreign military visitors. She doesn't have any details; she only knows she's helping with counter-espionage activities. I think I told you that her late husband was a military attaché, so she's been a really good asset, carrying on her late husband's role, more or less. I'm sure I can get her to agree to let you spend some time there so you can set up your radio and direction finder in some obscure room in her manor house. That will let you get some solid evidence on your suspicion about the Major's place."

"That's no suspicion, it's a fact as far as I'm concerned," said Tony, "and I'm not sure we should do that."

"Why? It's a perfect situation," said Bill.

"True, but I think it would be…" Tony paused.

"Spit it out, what's on your mind?"

"I'm just concerned that if the Major figures out that I'm spending an inappropriate amount of time there it will create serious suspicion."

"I think the most he'd think is that you're having an affair. Which would be a perfect explanation. Just come and go between here and there so it will be indicative of that. I'll call her and get it all squared away, well, not the affair part."

Tony and Bill sat with eyes locked for a few moments. Tony broke a smile, "Bill you're a son of a bitch!"

"Just doing my job, putting the best resources on the toughest problems," Bill replied, grinning.

"You said you had something else to tell me?

Bill nodded, "Yes, you'll really appreciate this one. I saved it for last. Second Officer Petra Wilkinson is an MI5 officer. They put her in Bletchley as an internal security monitor. They wanted someone on the inside to pick up rumor and gossip, look for vulnerabilities, and so on. Washington tells me, don't repeat this, that the Brits have some suspicion that ULTRA level intel has found its way into Russian hands. As you might guess, they are paranoid about keeping Bletchley's mission uncompromised, not to mention sensitive intel in general. She's been deeply involved in MI5's investigation of the deaths of Molly Lawson and Moira O'Riordan. They recalled Petra to London temporarily to head up the case on the Doctor. I think she wants him more than you do!"

Wembley Park Flat
London

Tony returned to his London flat after getting his gear from his cottage near Bletchley. He tossed his jacket on the bed and went into the bathroom, washed his hands, held a wash cloth under the hot water spigot and put the wash cloth on his face. He let it linger, savoring the invigoration of the heat on his face after the open air trip in the jeep. The phone on the nightstand next to his bed rang. He quickly toweled his face and ran to the phone. "Hoped I would catch you, my conference room, in an hour and a half," said Bill. Tony got himself together and headed for the embassy.

Bill was standing just inside the door of the conference room, "Mike, I'd like you to meet Lieutenant Commander Tony Romella. Tony, Mike Nelson."

"My pleasure Mike," said Tony.

"Likewise," said Mike in a strong deep voice and with a powerful handshake. Everything about Mike sent a tough message. He was about 6'6", with a pockmarked face, square jaw, generally sharp features, two-inch scar on his left forehead, bald, broad shoulders and brusque manner. Mike could well have been introduced as a gangster and Tony would not have been surprised.

"MI5 will be along any minute," said Bill, "How about some coffee or tea? Have a seat gentlemen."

"Coffee, black, please," said Mike.

"Touch of milk for me, or black," said Tony.

A Yeoman standing by the coffee mess at the back of the room promptly served their coffee in standard Navy ceramic mugs. Tony had his back to the conference door when he heard it open and close. He turned toward the door and smiled at what he saw, "Second Officer Petra Wilkinson, fancy that!" he called across the room.

Petra smiled, "Fancy indeed Commander, nice to see you again."

Bill got things underway, "We have some ground to cover and it's been a long day. Petty Officer, please serve the Second Officer what she needs, then close the door and hold my calls." Bill took the chair at the end of the table, Tony sat to his right; Petra and Mike took chairs on Bill's left.

"Tea please, thank you," said Petra.

The door closed firmly behind the petty officer. Bill began, "All right people, the classification of this conversation is Top Secret, U.S./U.K. eyes only. The purpose of this meeting is to set up a coordinating body that will meet at least weekly to share, plan and inform each other of our progress. OK, Petra, you're up," said Bill.

Petra opened a file folder, "Well, let's review the lot of it. We have intercepted many transmissions from the Doctor, so named by Tony I'm told, which suits our purpose. In the last day or so, and thanks to our mobile DF van and the bearings taken by the Commander, we are now quite certain that most transmissions are coming from a Russian Embassy's residential property in the outer reaches of London. The suspected second location that some transmissions are coming from is a building we've been watching. The linking of the Doctor's transmissions to the murders at Bletchley is made firm by reason of decyphered transmissions to and from the Doctor and a German handler in France, probably in the Lorient or Paris areas, but the location evidence is not conclusive. We're working on getting some HUMINT confirmation on that. Now then, recently, the Doctor specifically named Molly and Moira as terminated targets. We have begun breaking their cypher promptly. It's laborious and done only by hand. With all the other priorities for the U.S. and Bletchley analysts' time, they will do their best. Washington's helping with this task and it is greatly appreciated."

"You know?" Tony opined, "It strikes me odd that the handler would be in Lorient, or Paris for that matter, as opposed to Berlin. I can't help thinking that it could be part of an effort to support Admiral Dönitz's task to destroy Allied shipping to Britain, since Dönitz moved to the Lorient area from Paris. Coincidences always beg further analysis. German interest in Bletchley is due no doubt of its cover story being a government communications training center. Bletchley is seen as a potential source for the merchant marine crypto materials, procedures, engineering and so on. The Germans apparently have one source for some or all of that since they broke the cipher twice, but another source would be supplementary or backup."

Mike seized the opportunity of a pause, "Damn German spy in the Russian Embassy, ain't that a kick in the ass! They are walking on a high tight rope without a net. Petra, what about normal embassy personnel surveillance, anything turn up there?"

Petra shrugged, "We're not sure it's the Major. Could be his wife, so keep an open mind. And they were not a high priority up until two days ago. Those times when the Major and his wife were being watched, nothing significant was reported. Just travel to and from that manor house and the embassy, also a few places in and around London proper. Most seemed purely social or otherwise routine in nature. One thing about Tony's work with his portable DF," Petra continued, "it's been very valuable in clarifying the transmitter locations. I'd like to see that continue so that we can detect any new transmitters and new locations, should there be more than one agent. Any luck with Havenwood Bill?"

"I spoke with Lady Watson earlier. The long story made short, she's happy to help us out anyway she can. She has a large room, about 12x12, on her top floor that's got a few pieces of art and furniture stored in it, but she'll clear it out sufficiently to make a bedroom and work area for Tony. Lady Watson will make any furnishings available he needs and the room will not be accessible to the manor staff unless he requests otherwise, for linen service and the like. He can sanitize the room for those occasions. The cover story she and I came up with, with your approval, is that he's helping Lady Watson write a historical account of her husband's career in military intelligence. The staff will be told that those are private writings that will require British and U.S. government clearance before publication, thus the need for privacy."

"Quite nice of Lady Watson and quite plausible cover. I like it," said Petra, "While we're on that subject, we liked Tony's idea about the modified bandwidth radio and wire recorder to capture the high speed signals. Bletchley staged a few of them around London. I just happen to have one for you to take to Havenwood Tony."

Tony nodded enthusiastically.

Bill looked at Mike, "Your thoughts?"

Mike took in a deep breath, put his fingers together and cracked his knuckles with a loud crunch that sounded painful. "I have gone through the information that Scotland Yard shared with MI5 about what they developed regarding the victims, friends and associates and so forth. There does not appear to be any common denominator in all of that—frustrating. Well, except for Tony."

"Not funny Mike," said Tony with a smile as they all laughed.

Mike continued, "Sorry about that. The Yard also questioned people at the places the victims were known to have gone when off duty. They came up dry on that too, no possible enemies, unfriendly people, acquaintances that could be suspect, the works. Either the Doctor, or more likely an agent under his control, is damn clever in taking advantage of the standard security vulnerabilities of women at Bletchley. One thing for sure, this Doctor, or his agent, is a very clever person who has been extraordinarily careful about not being seen with the victims. Now that we have a suspicion that they are connected, strangely I might add, with both the Russian Embassy and the German spy network, our task has been made somewhat complex." Mike planted his elbows on the table and rubbed his hands over the barely visible gray stubble on his head.

Bill scanned his notepad and looked up, "Just for Mike and Tony's clarification, MI5 is in control of this effort," his eyes moved around the table and settled squarely on Petra, "we will do all we can to help you."

"Smashing! And please, all of you, call me Petra. We will be working too closely to attend formalities." Petra ran her fingers back through her hair, "Gentleman, MI5 is pleased with your participation in this operation." Petra scanned their faces briefly as she collected her thoughts. "Thank you for that, now as a minimum let's meet here every Friday at half three to reflect collectively upon the week and plan the following week's work, yes?" She looked around the table collecting nods of agreement. She turned to Tony, "Right, get us set up at Havenwood quickly so we can get some DF and recordings. Also, if you feel comfortable with it, do some recon on the estate to determine the physical security. If there's any opportunity to get a bug in there, we would probably do it."

"Roger that. I can be there and operating by tomorrow afternoon," said Tony. Bill gave a thumbs up.

Petra's attention then went to Mike, "Right, can you stake out the Russian estate? Log comings and goings, shadow people that leave there, yes? If at all possible, get others on the case, so you can tail more than one at a time. You know what we're looking for." She paused for his acknowledgement.

Mike gave a sharp nod, "Can do. I have already cased the exit from the estate and the routes they take in and out of there. I have identified all their vehicles and license plates. I'll pass all that on tomorrow. There's a great place to hide at an intersection they all go through where traffic coming in behind them won't be suspicious."

Petra smiled, "OK, MI5 will put at least two people on the Russian Embassy to do the same." She tore a note paper into small pieces and began writing a number down on each piece. "If anyone comes up with anything good, call me immediately. If I'm not there, tell them Nottingham is calling and leave a number where you can be reached. They'll know to get those messages to me, yes?"

"How about walkies?" asked Bill.

"No, they could intercept our radios," said Petra. "I don't want them to have any hint of us at this point anyway."

"Absolutely," said Tony, "If they have an intercept operation at their embassy, manor house or that garage, they'll hear them."

Mike interjected, "They've probably been hearing my guys. We have been using walkies all along, but we're using code words that have meanings that change daily. We even have preplanned dummy messages being sent by various members afield to cover the real traffic. Probably making them nuts if they are intercepting."

Bill smiled and looked down blankly at his lined pad of notes, rubbed his chin and thought for a moment, "So, Mike can get tipped off of something hot, but I'm concerned that one of you will run into something urgent or get into some sort of trouble and won't be able to tip us off."

Petra smiled wryly, "The nature of the beast Captain. Walkie-talkies are too big and too overt to go skulking around with for some of us. But, I'll come up with a short set of code words that we can include in innocent conversation that any of us can call in by phone. Not many words to the lot and something we can memorize and not have to carry with us on paper. I'll get that to you all by the end of the day. Anyone needing to use a code word will call that number I gave you. Memorize it and don't carry it with you. My staff or I will make sure that your contact is passed to me and Bill immediately." She glanced at her watch, "Gentlemen, ta ta, I have to accompany Sir David Petrie, our DG, to a briefing for Churchill at the Cabinet War Rooms and a car is waiting."

13 NIGHT WORK

Havenwood Estate

The butler and maid helped Tony move his seabag and heavy foot locker into a corner suite on the third floor. Inga decided to put Tony in what was once the private third floor office of her late husband. The staff found Lady Watson's explanation about Tony's presence and locked suite intriguing, but showed no particular curiosity beyond that. As professional domestic staff, they understood and respected privacy. Even though Tony had only spent a small amount of time at Havenwood, the staff found him congenial and they easily took him into their charge.

Tony removed and unrolled the clothes from his seabag and put them in a tall cherry wood armoire and tallboy dresser.

There was a knock on the door, followed by Inga's soft voice, "Coming down for tea?"

Tony opened the door, "Absolutely, I missed lunch getting organized in London and making the ride out here. I'm famished."

"Poor dear, you should have said something when you arrived! Don't be shy, speak up," she said, "Do you need anything else for the suite?"

"No, the butler and maid have outfitted me well."

"Right. Good on them. By the way, here's the key for the doors. May I come in? I want to show you something."

"Thank you, of course," he said and followed her to a narrow door on the outside corner of the suite.

"Same key for the front and this door, the spare key is safe in my room, none in the hands of any of the staff," she said then pointed at a door in the corner of the room. "Behind this door is a private spiral stairway that goes down to an outside exit opposite the stable. It's quite narrow and steep, so mind your feet, those steps can be tricky." She opened the door and motioned for him to take look.

"This may come in handy, thank you!" he said.

When Inga left, he stood by the window looking out to the rear of the estate and marveled at the wide range of experiences this assignment in London was providing. Being here at Havenwood was probably as good as it could get in a war. Tony felt quite the aristocrat with a three room suite, and a staff at his beck and call. Not to mention a well-appointed stable. Taking meals and tea with Lady Watson would surely be pleasant as well. He smiled.

At 1 a.m. Tony turned off the short-wave radio direction finder he set up in the sitting room of his suite. He wiped his palms over his ears. They were sweaty from several hours of wearing headphones and listening intently but in vain for the Doctor to transmit. After drying his hands and the ear pieces on his t-shirt, he pondered the disappointment of not hearing from the good Doctor. All transmissions in the past were heard between 10:00 p.m. and 11:30 p.m., so there was no likelihood of hearing him any more tonight. He slouched down on a crimson velvet love seat and rested his head on a dark green silk cushion. His eyes closed to better conjure images as he thought through how he might reconnoiter the Russian estate adjoining Inga's property. The love seat was too comfortable; nodding off was not a luxury he could afford right now. He put on his khaki uniform, boondockers, foul weather jacket, black gloves and a navy knit watch cap. A container of charcoaled grease paint in one hand, he smiled into the mirror as he imagined his blackened face. As his fingers were about to dip into the black it struck him that being discovered by a staff member in camouflage would be harder to explain than just being outside taking air. He took a six cell flashlight from his foot locker and rigged it with the red filter from the accessory compartment at the end of the flashlight barrel. Tony checked the lock on his suite's front door and quietly descended the private spiral staircase. Stepping out carefully onto the crushed stone adjacent to the stable made more noise than he expected. He quietly shut and locked the staircase door and took in a deep breath of dense humid air in a dark overcast night. The rush of biting cold through his nostrils hurt the tissue deep into his nose and gave him a momentary headache. He forced himself to breathe more slowly. The crimson rays of his flashlight allowed him to move at a quick pace along the path in the eerily quiet woods that led toward the Russian manor house. The only sounds he heard were those of his boots crushing leaves, branches and dirt under foot and animals scurrying and warning others of his presence. He came to the little Stonehenge then carefully moved in a half crouch through the brush toward the Russian property.

Tony turned off the flashlight and crawled the last 20 feet toward the fence that bounded the Russian property. The fence consisted of five-foot tall gray granite stone pylons spaced about eight feet apart. The side faces of the pylons had three equally spaced holes in which roughly hewn logs were secured. When he was close to the fence, he covered the flashlight lens with his fingers and slowly opened two fingers to let a hint of light through. There appeared to be neither wires running along the fence or a worn path along the perimeter. There was a dim slit of light peeking around blackout curtains in some rooms of the Russian manor house, perhaps fifty yards away. He recalled from pictures taken by Mike that it had two gray stone walled stories set on about the same size foundation as Lady Watson's house. Tony observed a sentry posted outside the rear door at the middle of the house. The sentry was sitting on an unpainted straight back wooden chair that was leaned back against the side of the house; a Mauser C96 automatic weapon laid across his lap. Tony remained prone and quiet, watching, listening in the dead silence and near total darkness. Thirty yards off the rear of the house was a barn, now garage, with a large sedan parked just outside. He recognized the distinctive long hood and general outline of a gray Duesenberg sedan barely visible from the diffuse light from a small bare bulb above the back door of the manor house. There were faint glints on parts of the chrome grille. The Russians honored the rule of blackout curtains, yet they felt the back door security was exempt for obvious reasons. Tony figured the British commandeered the sedan from the Germans when they left their embassy in a rush. Maybe the Russians somehow got the British to let them use it. Perhaps it came with the manor house, which he learned had previously, but briefly, been used by German diplomats. He also noticed that the barn doors were ajar showing what appeared to be a truck grille which generated some curiosity.

A Russian soldier came out of the back door of the house, slung his automatic weapon over his shoulder, struck a match off his boot sole, lit up a cigarette and chatted briefly with the soldier in the chair, who also lit a cigarette as they talked. The soft red glows at the tips of their cigarettes were visible in the dim light of the small bulb that softly illuminated the smoke they exhaled. After a few minutes, the soldier on the chair stood, ground his cigarette embers on his boot heel, put the stub of the remainder of the cigarette into his jacket pocket and went into the house. The guard had changed. Tony positioned his flashlight to illuminate his watch, pointed it away from the manor house, turned it on briefly and noted the time. The relieving sentry took his place on the chair, leaned back and got comfortable. In less than a half hour, the chin of the sentry fell down to his chest as he succumbed to the sandman.

After traveling the entire perimeter fence around the Russian property, making mental measurements of each leg, Tony retraced his path through the woods and returned to Inga's house. He tried to be quiet as he climbed the private stairway up to his room but it seemed that each plank creaked underfoot. He was halfway between the second and third floor when he heard a door open behind him. He turned and directed his flashlight back down the stairs. Inga was leaning slightly out of the door to her suite. "Keeping bloody late hours Commander!" she whispered in a jesting tone.

"I'm sorry Inga, I tried to step lightly," said Tony.

"No worries, I'm a light sleeper," she said, "I was reading, in fact I was just pouring a spot of brandy to help me get back to sleep when I heard you. Do you fancy a nightcap?"

"Oh that's very kind of you, but, it's 4 a.m. …"

She didn't let him finish, "It's bloody good Spanish brandy, VSOP, and you're not intruding, come have some, for uh good health, yes?" she whispered and motioned.

"I will join you shortly Inga, I must get cleaned up and presentable," he said, shining the flashlight on his face.

He went up to his room, tossed his jacket, gloves and hat on a chair. He put on some clean khaki pants and shirt and street shoes. He returned to her door on the spiral stair and knocked softly. It was open slightly.

"Come in, come in.". There were two stuffed chairs sitting somewhat near the fireplace in the sitting room. They were angled toward the fire, with a mahogany round table between them. A decanter of brandy and two snifters were waiting on the table. A crystal chandelier with several candles hung over the table bathing the room with a dull amber glow. Inga was sitting in one of the chairs with her bare feet tucked up alongside her, white brocade slippers were sitting on the floor in front of her chair. She was wearing what could only be defined as elegant sleepwear. It was an ankle length white on white multilayered night gown supported by thin straps over the shoulder. A light shawl of the same material was draped over her shoulders.

"Quite an improvement," she said grinning at him as he sat down, "pour us a nightcap, yes?"

When she turned and leaned to take her glass and toast a short war, his eyes could not escape the cleavage revealed by the deep V in her nightgown. "Have I embarrassed you?" she asked.

He blushed profusely, "Frankly, it's stunning," he said, wondering why the hell he said that. The words just seemed to come from a place he could not control.

She smiled widely, "I could tell." Now she was blushing. "Are you comfortable up there? Anything we need?"

"I'm fine. It's very gracious of you to help."

"No trouble at all, I rather enjoy the company," she said, taking a long sniff of the brandy and savored a sip. "Visiting the neighbor were we?"

"Yes and all is well."

"Pleased to hear it," she quipped as she got up. "Come, sit by the fire and get warm." They sat down on the leopard skin rug in front of the fireplace. He sat cross-legged, she was leaning down on one elbow, brandy in the other hand.

Tony could feel his heart beat quickening. She was charming and elegant -- more than charming and elegant. She extended her glass toward him, "To the bloody Yanks," she toasted.

"To the plucky Brits" he toasted. They touched glasses and laughed. Their eyes locked for a few moments in silence. Only their minds knew what was exchanged in those fleeting moments. Whatever it was created butterflies in his stomach. They talked about horses, fox hunting, medieval art and classical music. Tony realized that a fork in the road was fast approaching. Either they would wind up in each other's arms or he would use his better judgement. Each path had its good and bad side. Tony took his final sip, "You were right, very fine brandy, now I need to get some sleep. Thank you for your hospitality Inga."

She took his snifter and set it beside hers on the hearth, "It pleases me that you enjoyed it. I enjoyed our conversation. I feel I know you so well. Have we met in another life?"

The next night was absent of any moon. Tony crawled quietly into position to observe the Russian sentry at the back door of their mansion. He expected the timing and behavior of the guards to be the same as the previous night. He waited for the change of sentries. It had been a pleasant but uneventful two days, but with disappointment that nothing was heard from the Doctor. Every day the Doctor is free to operate is another day he could have done harm. Tony's mind went to full alert when the mansion back door opened and the guard's relief came out. Tony glanced over to the garage; the sliding doors were wide open. The sedan was visible just inside, next to the truck. His heart began beating a little faster and harder.

Tonight he had to be more daring. Earlier that afternoon, Mike, disguised as a postman, delivered a box addressed to Tony. Tony took it to his room and studied the contents: a small black backpack, electronic equipment, operating instructions and handwritten orders from Captain Taylor. Once read and understood, the orders were crumpled and burned in the fireplace.

The Russian soldiers talked for a few minutes while they smoked, then one retired. The remaining soldier smoked his cigarette to a mere nub and crushed it under the sole of his tall black boot. He wandered over to the garage and went inside. Tony strained to see what the soldier was up to. He heard the squeaky door of the truck open, then shut. The soldier reappeared at the garage doorway and lifted a wine bottle to his mouth. Perfect, thought Tony. That wine will help him along to slumber land. Once the soldier leaned back against the mansion wall in his chair, weapon across his legs and belly full of wine, he quickly fell fast asleep. Tony crawled a little further down the fence line, then over to the wall of the garage and along the wall toward the front where he could peek around the corner at the sentry. He crawled quickly around the corner and moved into the garage. He went past the rear of the truck to the side of the sedan. He took off his backpack and pulled out one of the small wire recorders Mike had provided. It had four hours of recording time, but activated only in the presence of sound. He crawled under the car and magnetically attached the recording device to the floorboard under the rear passenger seat.

14 WHERE IS THE DOCTOR?

U.S. Naval Attaché Office
London

Mike Nelson and Petra Wilkinson were already in the conference room when Bill and Tony entered. They all exchanged handshakes, nods and pleasantries. "OK Tony, give us an update," said Bill.

"Well, I think I bring you a gift, but it remains to be seen," said Tony as he reached into a leather pouch and pulled out two small reels of wire. "I was able to plant the wire recorder under the rear floorboard of the Duesenberg at the Russian estate. These are the first two reels recorded on it, I dated them with the nights I removed them. It appears that the reel from last night has recorded the most, about 3 hours or so, judging from the amount of wire on it. The night before looks to be about half that. That three hour reel would be more than a round trip to their embassy, so this could be interesting stuff. Their security is surprisingly relaxed out there, at least during the dark hours."

Mike clapped his hands together making a loud report, "That's terrific; I'll get this transcribed and get copies to you all by tomorrow morning. I'll get you more reels Tony. If there's anything on these recordings that might warrant our attention sooner, I'll call each of you."

"OK," said Tony, "I've got two radio intercepts of the Doctor, both were booming signals and unquestionably coming from next door. Both were reported to the intercept site as previously arranged."

Petra nodded, "Quite. MI5 plotted the line bearings and they indicate you're right about being from the Russian estate. There has only been one signal sent from that second location in the past week. We can't think of a proper reason why they'd transmit from two locations. Bloody puzzle that. We're still waiting on Bletchley's report of the success on decyphering those messages. Hopefully, one of these messages will give us some hint of what's going on at that second location."

Tony sat back to listen to what the others had to report.

"Well, we have kept a close eye on the Major and his wife," said Mike. "She sure seems to be more than just the Major's wife. She appears to have an operational role at the embassy. Her papers don't reflect that, but she doesn't stay home and mind the store. Granted there's no kids, but still."

Tony grinned, "OK, I've taken a look at the dates and times of the Doctor's transmissions and compared them with the whereabouts of the Major and his wife at those times. They were both at the manor house in each case, except for the signal from the second location, and she was out of the manor house at the time. And, as it would happen, she slipped the tail we had on her during that absence. I hoped it would give us a hint at which of them is transmitting or if someone else in there is doing it. She's clearly involved though. How about decrypts of the Doctor's traffic? Any more success on that at Bletchley or in Washington?" He looked alternately at Bill and Petra. Tony sensed Petra knew something but shrugged.

Bill sat forward and referred to his notes, "Washington has reported success. I should have a full report of all decrypts by tomorrow afternoon."

"We are doing the same thing at Bletchley," said Petra, "and I think that the way is being cleared to share and exchange the more sensitive intelligence on this case with Washington and thus your offices as we speak. We should be able to break them all post haste since the priority has been raised.

Bill smiled, "Excellent, between the two of us, we shouldn't miss anything. I think we're making significant progress,"

"Right," said Petra, "tickety-boo here. Let's adjourn until tomorrow afternoon so we can review the latest data. We'll have better ideas on what the next moves should be."

When the group met again they had plenty of information to analyze.

"So, the fact is, we still don't know whether the Doctor is the Major or his wife, or some third person, yes?" asked Petra as she skimmed through Mike's report.

"Correct," said Mike, "The recent transmissions have all been heard at night and both the Major and his wife have been in their manor house in each instance. I've had the estate under constant surveillance day and night. The second location seems to have gone quiet, radio-wise."

Petra nodded, "Well, we don't have any evidence on who the Doctor is or whether he's acting alone or with one or more others. The plain texts of the Doctor's messages don't give us a clear statement of the sex of the drafter either. I went so far as having a psychologist go through the bloody things this morning, looking for subtle hints of gender."

Mike added, "They have changed from being overt to more clever about how they disguise who they are targeting. That's troubling in itself. Their targets, locations and sources are given very nondescript code names. Our analysts say they appear to have three targets under consideration. We have to assume that one or more of them will get snuffed at some point if they fail to cooperate."

"Spot on," said Petra, "our thinking, based on the message plain texts, is that these targets have not been directly approached by the Doctor. We have no idea where these targets may be located or anything about them. We've had the embassy under constant surveillance. There have been instances when each of them left the embassy independent of the other for different periods of time, but we haven't had people available to tail them fully without sacrificing embassy surveillance. We're trying to solve that." Captain Taylor looked at Mike with frustration plainly evident.

"Don't look at me Bill," said Mike, "the embassies are MI responsibility. Besides, we don't have the people right now to do it either but I'm working on it. The major or his wife are not the person shadowing or contacting the targets and doing the killing, in my opinion. They may lead us to that person, however. There's at least one other agent we need to identify and fast."

Petra thought deeply for a moment, "I think we have enough evidence in front of us today to sort that out. Tony, did you notice how it appeared that the Doctor was told to report in advance when he was going to make contact with a target?"

"Yes. It looks like they are sensitive to the attention the murders have gotten. Hopefully, we'll be able to get in front of them on the next contact," said Tony.

Petra nodded, "Right."

Mike shrugged and showed his frustration, "So, why don't we just neutralize both of them?"

"Bloody hell, don't we all want that!" said Petra, grinning. "I would bloody well be up against the wall getting that one by the DG." They all laughed.

"At this point, do we still need Tony at Havenwood?" asked Bill, looking around the table.

Mike shrugged his shoulders, "We may get better intel on these guys from more wire recordings."

"I read the transcripts carefully," said Petra, "They are being extremely careful about what they say, probably for the driver's sake, so," Petra hesitated a moment, "I don't think it's worth the risk of the Germans seeing him there so much, affair notwithstanding," she smiled. "Also, we have all the direction finding info we need. I say get that wire recorder off that car and bring Tony back to London." Mike nodded.

Bill leaned forward, "OK, Tony, arrange to get your stuff out of Havenwood.? He turned to Petra, "Question is, what's our plan now?"

She cleared her throat softly, "Mike, you and I need to coordinate getting some tails on the Major's wife when she leaves the manor or embassy. I think this is a case where we just have to take action and let the bloody politics catch up later. She's been wary and very slippery. Between the two of us, we might keep a better eye on her."

"Affirmative Petra, lets meet after this," said Mike.

Petra nodded and turned to Bill, "I have an idea, let's use Tony to help figure out how they are identifying their targets. I would guess that the Doctor probably has an agent near Bletchley Park feeding him info."

Tony added, "Exactly, the Doctor has someone blending in, at a pub perhaps, anywhere people meet and talk, the cafeteria at Bletchley, who knows? Since I know what the Major and his wife look like, I'd recognize them instantly and he knows that. So, it's not going to be one of them."

"Between our combined resources we should be able to get pictures of all the Russian embassy staff," said Petra. "If they don't have someone from the civilian population up there helping them, heaven forbid, then it stands to reason that it would be a Russian embassy employee."

Tony leaned back and drew in a deep breath, "Well, it could also be a covert German agent that infiltrated. There's only three pubs that most Bletchley staff frequent," said Tony. "Molly and Moira, God rest their souls, were both living in quarters near enough to Bletchley that they didn't require transportation all the time and used the base transport only when it was convenient or in nasty weather. Thus, they frequented the two pubs that are closest to the base. It won't be too hard to figure out who in those pubs is out of place if we look hard."

Bill took a deep breath, "Oh how I hate the idea of going to Winant to expedite getting Tony back to Bletchley. Captain Hardcastle will have a damn fit."

"I can help with that," said Petra, "In fact, I'll take care of getting us back. The MOD probably has enough reason to justify making Hardcastle privy to some level of our assignment so he won't interfere. Since we were there before, it won't be too odd to the other chaps at the base. We'll stagger our return a couple days apart. We can't wait longer than that."

110

Tony walked back to Bill's office with him. An urgent cable was brought to Bill by his Yeoman. He read it and looked up, "Good grief Tony, the Japanese are expected to take Singapore within 24 hours. At any rate, I'm glad we decided to keep your cottage at Bletchley," said Bill, "I hoped we'd get you back there." Bill took a cigar from a fancy wooden box, lit it and settled back in his chair. "

"Somewhere in all this cloak and dagger work, spend as much time as you can spare to detect awareness of Operation Chariot in that high command traffic to Dönitz. Also, Washington wants us to advise them promptly on any follow-up on the Merchant crypto compromise. And for God's sake try and find an opportunity to get the Cigar data. The ambassador has really been on my ass about it, in a nice way. I assured him we'd be back on it as soon as we could get you back to Bletchley."

15 CIGARS AND FISH

A Block
Bletchley Park

Tony was concentrating on FISH decrypts between Berlin and Admiral Dönitz looking for references pertinent to the imminent Operation Chariot and intelligence about Allied convoys. He was so immersed in the analysis that he was surprised to realize Petra was tapping his shoulder repeatedly.

"Pardon me, are you at a point where you can take a wee break?" she asked with a smile.

"Oh, sure," he laughed, "I just saw where the Berlin told Dönitz to pull the wolfpacks off of Y147 due the threat of the escorting tin cans. The convoy has no threats between them and port now. Did Marion go home?"

"Indeed she has, it's half seven and she was here early," said Petra.

"Half seven? Where did the day go? Time for a bite?" asked Tony.

"Well yes, but first, while Marion isn't in the office, I want to talk strategy," said Petra with a serious face. "This morning I had a chat with some chaps in MI5 and we came up with a plan, but you have to go along with it."

"There's a saying in the Navy, don't volunteer for anything," joked Tony.

She interrupted with a solemn look, "Right, let's be serious now. I want to give this a go. Here's the plan. MI5 thinks merely identifying someone we suspect of being the Doctor's agent doesn't necessarily solve the problem. While MI5 and Mike's people are proving or disproving the suspect's identity, the real agent can terminate another uncooperative target from Bletchley. So far, the victims have been relatively low level personnel and didn't have any significant vulnerability to blackmail. Here's where we come in. We, as officers, could be seen as higher value targets with significant vulnerability and if we were to innocently offer ourselves up, we could possibly redirect the agent's attention from the three potential targets found so far."

He jumped in at a pause, "Oh that sounds like a stretch of the imagination. And us? How?"

She laughed, "I said be serious, bloody hell! I think we all can control this since we are informed and have protection resources that the victims did not have. They didn't cooperate, but we could, to some degree and thus set the trap for the agent."

He shook his head, "I have to admit, I'm not sure where you're going with this. So, have you all figured out how," he emphasized the word, "we make ourselves attractive targets that get the agent's attention? Dare I ask?"

She grinned, "Right, we make him think we're having an affair."

"Oh my God, you're not serious Petra, you and me?"

"Just put yourself in his place, Tony. He'll learn, from listening to our little act, that I'm a married officer at Bletchley whose husband is away doing his duty and you are the single Yank doing what single Yanks do with birds. If they don't do extensive research and learn that I'm actually a war widow, they won't see the ruse. They'll be focused on my vulnerabilities."

Tony was shaking his head, "Our reputations will suffer with the others at Bletchley if it becomes obvious and Captain Hardcastle will just…"

She interrupted, nodding, "Right, but Hardcastle can be handled. This will require some coordination and good acting on our part," she said, "we'll have to behave accordingly in the pubs, just don't be a Yank and take it seriously, yes?"

They stared at each other for what seemed minutes. "OK, it's worth a try," said Tony. "Does Captain Taylor and Mike know about this ingenious plan?"

She laughed, "Quite! Let's head to the canteen for that bite."

Two Evenings Later
Livingston's Lion's Pride Pub
Near Bletchley Park

Hardcastle wasn't very happy about it but came around after being briefed on enough of the developments to stay out of the way. Inspector Hale and his Chief Inspector had also been taken into some semblance of confidence by MI5 so that Scotland Yard would not interfere. The plot was in motion.

This was Tony and Petra's second night and as many pubs in their search plan for suspicious pub goers. Tony looked over when he heard the solid thud of the rustic wood pub door. It was Petra, arriving about twenty minutes after Tony. He waved his hand high over the busy crowd to get her attention. "Good evening Second Officer Wilkinson," said Tony as she approached, motioning to a stool beside him.

"Good evening Lieutenant Commander Romella. Fancy meeting you here," she said, placing her hat on the bar. He held the shoulders of her navy overcoat as she twisted out of it and took her seat. Tony hung her hat and coat over his on one of the wall pegs.

Tony returned and sat beside her, "I got lucky, it's warmer down this end of the bar by the fireplace. Your stool just came open and I've been telling everyone who dared claim it that I was holding it for someone. What can I get you?"

"I think tonight a Newcastle Brown would be lovely," she said.

He got the barkeeper's attention, "A Guinness and a Newcastle Brown please."

She smiled, "Gotten accustomed to our warm beer have we?"

He laughed and noted that she had removed the pins in her hair that held it all in check. It was now flowing down close to her shoulders, "Aye, Guinness has a unique body and flavor, I've developed quite a taste for it." He leaned over close to her ear and whispered, "There's a guy standing in the corner over your left shoulder that is worth observing. I've seen him here before on several occasions. He hasn't said a word to anyone. Never does."

Just then the radio announcer interrupted music on the hour for a news update. The first topic captured Tony's attention when they mentioned that German submarines were beginning to attack merchant shipping off the coast of the United States. She also listened carefully. They looked at each other showing their surprise that the information had become public. The news summary ended and the program returned to dance music. She looked at him with a coy smile and said, "I'd love a dance and a chat about happier things, what do you say Yank?"

"Smashing!" he said with a broad smile.

She took his hand as they moved to the dance area. He grasped her right hand and put his other hand around her waist, maintaining a proper distance. She slowly moved in closer, placed her head alongside his and whispered, "He's dressed like a Scot, but my gut says he bloody well isn't." To Tony's surprise, she came closer and cuddled into him as they danced on their small share of the open area in front of the fireplace. He put both hands on her waist and held her snugly, cheek to cheek. They moved among other couples also on the boards dancing. "Try to move us over closer to him," she whispered, "and don't forget, we're acting, Tony!"

He smiled and whispered back kiddingly, well, sort of kiddingly, "Oh that will be difficult."

She pulled her face back from his cheek, focused her blue eyes into his and with a stern look whispered, "Do control yourself love." He felt his face flush. The feel of her body against his and her modest but firm breasts against his chest was something he could get used to. Her softly attractive physical features, her intellect and her manner had all come together subtly over the time they worked together. She sneaked into his thoughts and captured his attention in a way he found unique. As they came within ear-shot of the Scot she said, "My husband would be furious about this, but it's a lovely diversion from the war, yes?"

He admired the imagination of her act and played along. He said with a boyish grin, "Well then, I won't tell him."

"You bloody well best not," she said cutely but emphatically. She whispered in his ear, "I didn't take any drama classes at university. Hopefully I'm not dreadful."

Tony chuckled softly and whispered back, "Olivia de Havilland couldn't have done better." As they moved away from the Scot, Tony said, "He appears to be studying us." They kept moving slowly through the others. "Petra, now that I've had a closer look, I do recall seeing that face before in the other pub," said Tony. "He definitely does not resemble any of the Russian Embassy staff photos. I studied those thoroughly."

"Quite. I think he's worth playing with," she said. "If he's working for the Doctor he'll be here again for the next couple nights and so will we."

"I can't think of a better way to lay a trap," he said with a devious grin.

"Don't be such a bloody Yank," she said with a wry smile. They danced a bit longer and continued the act of being chummy to set the stage.

They left the pub and after a brief hug and peck for the benefit of any observer, returned to their respective quarters.

The Mansion
Bletchley Park

The next morning Tony phoned Bill to update him on the activities of the prior evening at the pub as soon as he awoke.

Bill took it all in then said, "Excellent, we may have a break in this. Oh, By the way, I know you'll be interested in this. The Chariot raid was a total surprise, strategically a huge success, but the casualties were high. The exit plan for the commandos didn't quite work out as planned and they had to scramble and improvise. It looks like a third or so out of over 600 in the raid made it out, hopefully the rest are still escaping or were taken prisoner rather than KIA."

"Oh, I appreciate the update on that Bill, it was one damn interesting and daring operation. Those British commandos are tough buggers."

Tony called Mike when he hung up with Bill. "Hey Mike, It's Tony. I think we have a fish on."

Mike chuckled, "I think so too. Turns out we just started watching that guy. He's clever, that's for sure. One of my men spotted him a few nights ago in a pub and thought he was worth watching. We finally got someone assigned to him. They saw him arrive at the pub and follow you when you left the pub. The way your cottage sits, with the back wall not far from the edge of that little hedged alley, there was good cover for him to sneak up close to the cottage and not be seen. He can probably hear what goes on in your bedroom and living room pretty easily. Take note of that. He lurked outside your wall for about 10 minutes, then the slippery bastard used a series of evasions which resulted in our guy losing him. He's anything but a novice. I got the word to Petra also."

"That's good information Mike. We at least know what we're dealing with. We'll find a way to exploit this info Mike, thanks a ton!"

Livingston's Lion's Pride Pub
Near Bletchley Park

"It's 7:30, I'm surprised he's not here by now," Tony whispered in Petra's ear when she returned from the loo, "but the night is young. My turn, I'll be right back."

117

"Right! I'll get us another round," she said.

Two pints later, when Tony was about to suggest they call it a night, the pub door opened, "Speak of the devil," he muttered to Petra.

"That would be lovely," she said as their target passed close by on the way to a stool four down from theirs.

They merged into the Saturday night dancing crowd, probably half of them from Bletchley. He led her mainly around the edge of the dance area to occasionally pass within earshot of the Scot. The several drinks they had enjoyed while waiting for the Scot provided that borderline buzz of the mind that conjures pleasant thoughts. Her brunette curly locks flowed down below her ear lobes and tickled his ears and neck. "I sure look forward to Saturday night. One gets to look forward to not having to work the next day for a change," he said.

"Right! Finally, a day in the month we won't have to work. We all need our leisure time, yes?" Out of the corner of her eye, she noted the Scot was paying attention to them. "What do you plan to do tomorrow?" she asked.

"Sleep in as long as I can," he said

"Sounds splendid, perhaps I'll do the same," she said with a flirtatious set of accents and tone, then kissed his cheek.

He felt his face flush, which she was able to make happen so easily. After searching a bit for words he whispered, "He seems quite intrigued with us." His hands dropped to her waist and gently moved her closer until they were in a dancing hug, cheek to cheek. Now it was her face that flushed.

"Quite. Let's give him his due, yes?" she whispered into his ear. Then at normal voice, she said, "OK love, take me to that lovely cottage of yours."

He was glad he had purchased a small steamer trunk to stow his special gear out of sight from her or other prying eyes. It sat locked and inconspicuous in the small pantry off the kitchen.

According to the plan, Mike's agent tailed the Scot to Tony's cottage.

The agent observed the Scot slowly and carefully position himself close to Tony's cottage wall.

Tony and Petra spent a half hour role playing as two half-high flirts, building a fire, talking about brandy and being playful, at normal voice levels. They eventually moved to the bedroom, sat and moved on the bed in ways that, with mutterings and appropriate sounds, built a convincing scenario of love-making.

She whispered very softly, "Let's just be quiet for about an hour then I'll leave, yes?"

He nodded and stretched out along the edge of the bed. She sat on the other side of the bed. "That was rather fun," he whispered.

"Bloody Yank aren't we!" she whispered and poked him in the shoulder.

Tony drifted off under the calming effects of three pints of Ireland's finest dark beer. She laid back and napped involuntarily as well, waking in surprise. "Tony," she said chuckling, "I must away to my quarters for a proper rest. See you soon, love."

Later, at 6:00 am, the Doctor used his wireless radio outside of his usual schedule. Knockholt intercepted the message, Bletchley decyphered it and promptly reported the text to MI5. The information was promptly relayed to Petra, who contacted Bill, Mike and Tony. The Doctor told his contact that a new target of very high interest had been identified, assigned it number D2 and provided a summary description. The doctor further advised that he will proceed with making a contact. The summary was a dead ringer for Petra.

A Block
Bletchley Park

Marion was having a conversation with Petra when Tony came into the office. "Good morning Commander, glad you're here," said Petra, "Marion's not feeling well and I'm going to get a car from the motor pool while she's seeing the Park doctor and then take her home. I'll get some files out for you then would you mind the store please? If anyone comes knocking, I'll be about a half hour or so."

Tony could hardly believe this divine providence. This could be the day he gets his hands on the Project Cigar documents. "Of course! I hope you feel better Marion."

"Bit of a bad cold, my chest is just burning," said Marion.

"Take her home where she can get some rest Petra. Some tea and lemon perhaps. And we like to think chicken soup works wonders," said Tony.

Tony went right to work on the files Petra put on his desk. He waited for them to be gone for a while to be sure they wouldn't return for something one of them had forgotten. He stared at the vault door, still open. He looked at the office door and hoped nobody would come knocking. A chill ran up his spine as he entered the vault. The file cabinets were labeled by date range, country and military service. He located a cabinet marked DECEMBER 1941, Japan. In the third drawer he found a set of folders marked 'PEARL HARBOR'. His heart began pounding in his ears. Inside these folders was the collection of intercepts and messages relating to the attack on Pearl Harbor. He quickly rifled through the couple hundred or so documents, racing against the clock, knowing Petra could soon return. His eye caught something as he flipped through the papers. A strong subliminal urge forced him to stop and flip back a few pages. There it was. An intercept log of a katakana Morse intercept log marked in large block pencil letters, 'WINDS.' It caused his heart to skip a beat as he skimmed the innocuous weather report looking for the all too familiar code phrases. His eyes flew right to them -- HIGASHI NO KAZEAME and NISHI NO KAZE HARE with the pencil markings of EAST WIND RAIN and WEST WIND CLEAR. The technical information of the first intercept at Bletchley was also penciled along the margins of the typed page:

date, time, intercept operator, who was notified and when, etc., exactly what Tony needed. Mentally reliving the anguish this message first caused when he saw it on December 6th in his office in Washington caused a shiver to again race through his body. Learning the Japanese had initiated war plans against the U.S. and Britain was shocking then and seeing those coded phrases to that effect again renewed those feelings. Tony was glad that Bill was able to get a subminiature camera for him and that he had it in his jacket pocket.

Tony was busy analyzing decrypted messages when Petra returned.

"Poor dear was so embarrassed, she lost her brekky in the loo just before you came in," said Petra. "Thanks for minding the office."

"Not at all Petra, I'll soon be ready for the next lot when you get a chance."

Tony sat down at Marion's desk, picked up the phone and dialed Captain Taylor. Petra was busy pulling some documents requested urgently by Alan Turing, the renowned mathematician at Bletchley that Captain Hardcastle had correctly anticipated that Tony hoped to meet one day. Even though she was busy and not paying attention to him, he knew he needed to be circumspect with this call, "Bill, I have news about the cigars you were trying to get your hands on. I was able to find a box of them. I'll bring them to our next meeting."

"Excellent Tony, thank you. Listen, Lieutenant Ryan Jacob is going up there tomorrow on a courier run. I'll ask him to make an early departure so he can meet you in the canteen for breakfast. You can give the cigars to him. No telling when your next visit to London will be."

That afternoon Mike assigned a special protection team to covertly watch Petra's every move. It was assumed that she was the one the Doctor referred to as Case D2. It was a reasonable assumption that the Doctor would consider her being highly vulnerable to blackmail due to her apparent adultery. Mike's team was capable of eliminating the Scot or grabbing him, whatever was prudent in the course of events. They were in place as Tony and Petra continued their romance ruse that night.

The Scot was not at the pub when Tony and Petra arrived. He showed up nearly an hour later and nonchalantly took a seat near them. She took a closer look at his clothes in short glances over time. The Scot looked like something from a catalog of fine Scottish clothes. His heavy tweed coat, Balmoral cap, fisherman's knit sweater and worsted wool tartan trousers didn't have the slightest bit of weathered or worn look. As usual, his thin block-jawed face was sullen. He never smiled or said a word to anyone. He merely sipped a pint, watched and listened. Petra put on a classic act of getting just a little drunk during the next hour, getting a bit giddy, silly, happy and flirtatious. Tony skillfully and quite willingly played right into it. They danced and talked and took great advantage when near enough to the Scot for him to hear their teasing. "Tony love, it's bloody well time you took me home," she said. "Mind my stool love, I'll be right back." Out of the corner of his eye Tony noticed the Scot glance at her heading to the loo, then leave the pub.

They walked the half-mile to his cottage, her arm under his. It was chilly, as usual, with a half-moon that had a hazy corona. They whispered and laughed like a couple in a fresh romance. Anyone following them would have been soundly convinced of their involvement. The wooden gate in the cottage fence creaked and groaned as rust in the hinges grated. She started singing softly but giddily, exaggerating the words to the song, "By the Light of the Silvery Moon."

"Quiet dear, you'll wake the neighborhood," he scolded.

"It's the moon love, I can't help it," she said, clinging to his arm as he fussed with the key to open the door. He led her into the darkness inside. He closed and locked the door then turned on the floor lamp just inside. It cast a soft light into the room that served as a living and dining area. The blackout curtains were still pulled shut from the previous night. The large stone fireplace was cold and no help yet for the chill in the room. "I'd offer to sleep on the couch, but I don't have one," said Tony quietly.

She gave him a smirk, hung her coat on the wall hook next to his and whispered, "We'll be making do with the floor then won't we! OK, let's take the stage."

He snickered and said softly, "Oh what we go through for love of country." They assumed that an agent would go to great lengths to gather irrefutable information on personal vulnerability, such as adultery on her part, making blackmail an effective tool to gain cooperation. Tony and Petra carried out their deception for anyone who would get themselves into earshot of the cottage walls and windows in the dark of night.

"Tony love, get this fire going and pour us some of that splendid brandy you have," she said, rubbing her hands together for warmth.

"Have a seat on this nice thick rug in front of the fireplace Petra, I'll get things going here in a jiffy." He took kindling from the bucket by the fireplace, arranged it carefully in the fire pit, lit it with a wooden match from a box on the mantle and watched it for a moment. "Ah there we go," he said and placed two split logs from another bucket onto the burning kindling. "That should do it, we'll be toasty in no time at all," he said. "Now for the brandy." He took two brandy snifters from the mantle, poured a short ration into each from the wide-based glass ship's decanter on the mantle and handed a glass to Petra.

"Cheerio, love," she said emphatically.

"Cheerio, love," he mimicked playfully, "sitting there like that gives me a nice view of some great looking legs."

"Typical yank! Sit down next to me and drink your brandy! Tony, we bloody well must be discreet in all this, bloody hell. If the Captain finds out, it will be tally ho the fox! And then my husband will find out," she said.

"And, the Captain will have me back in London in the blink of an eye, then I'll get sacked and sent back to the States," replied Tony.

Their conversation meandered through contrived small talk between two flirts for a half hour.

"Brandy tastes so much better taken from your lips," he said as they sat grinning at each other, pleased with themselves for their improvisations.

"Does it now? Give some to me, love!" She paused then said, "Oh it does from yours as well!"

"Was that a shiver dear?" he asked. "Shall we retire to the comforts of a thick down comforter, wool sheets and body heat?"

"Spot on love."

As they approached the door to the bedroom, she whispered, "Self-control now Tony."

He laughed and whispered, "The bed is so squeaky, even I would be convinced." She punched him firmly in the ribs.

Petra slept comfortably on the bed through the night, while Tony slept, rather uncomfortably, wrapped in a goose down comforter on the floor in front of the fireplace. He didn't sleep very well, tossing and turning, adding a log periodically, until finally the break of dawn was detectable behind the dark curtains. He woke her so she could make her seemingly clandestine departure.

Canteen
Bletchley Park

The next morning Tony looked forward to breakfast at the Bletchley canteen. Thoughts of bangers, eggs and fried tomatoes whetted his appetite while he rode his newly acquired but old and somewhat rusty bike to the Park.

Tony and Jacob enjoyed breakfast and small talk. Then, with a parting handshake, one Minox camera was exchanged for another. Tony then went to his Mansion garage loft desk. He hung his hat and bridge coat on the clothes tree in the corner and walked to the little table on which sat the single phone shared by the loft analysts. He dialed Captain Taylor's direct line, "Good morning Captain, how's your day so far?

Bill chuckled, "So far it's going well, ask me in an hour or two. Have you had your breakfast?"

"Yes sir, I did. The Lieutenant and I had a fine English breakfast at the canteen. I gave him the box of cigars. You're going to love them."

"Thank you Tony, I'll have to share one with the ambassador. As you know, he likes them too. By the way, Mike was just here and gave me a good rundown on last night. The trout is eyeing two mayflies floating down the stream, their wriggling making circles on the water surface. Such a tempting lure it is."

"How about the Doctor? asked Tony.

"Nothing much new there," said Bill.

"Alright, we discussed several possible fishing trips," said Tony. "You'll get the details later."

"Be careful near the edge of the stream Tony, the banks are slippery."

"Will do," said Tony with a chuckle. He took a deep breath and let his mind digest the fact that Project Cigar, seemingly so risky and perhaps impossible, had been accomplished and was now a mere part of past activity and little further importance to him, especially in light of the involvement with MI5. He had been able to prove to President Roosevelt that the Brits had not withheld a warning of the attack on Pearl Harbor in order to get the U.S. into the war they were avoiding. He smiled; he loved his Navy life. Had he chosen a proprietor's life in Maine or a professorship in a university, he could never accomplish anything to compare with this life. He felt good.

16 CATCH AND RELEASE

Tony's Cottage

The next phase of the plan to entrap the Scot, or other agent assigned to make contact with Petra, was now in motion. Petra was traveling to London by herself, giving ample opportunity for the agent to confront her.

Tony looked at his watch for the umpteenth time. He figured Petra's bus should have just arrived in London's Piccadilly Square. Typical of Tony, nervous energy was being drained off by his habitual tapping of a pencil eraser on the table. A mental motion picture developed when he closed his eyes and put his head down on his arms. She's stepping off the double-decker bus. People are moving about in the moonlight with their coats closed tight up to their chins. The mental imagery suddenly disappeared as he slipped into a brandy induced nap. He awoke when he heard his phone ringing. He grabbed it and glanced at his watch. More than two hours had passed.

"Tony I have some news," said Captain Taylor, Tony's heart skipped a beat. "The trout swallowed the Mayfly. Mike is trying to land the fish now."

"My God Bill, any details?" asked Tony.

"It was a smooth grab Tony, really smooth. They obviously were watching her closely, waited for her to walk where nobody was close or paying attention, then put her into a car. They took off like a bat out of hell and proceeded to execute some skilled evasive driving and lost our tail. The car's plates were phony—dead end there. Mike's team never regained contact with the car."

"Damn it Bill are you saying they didn't get the bastards?" asked Tony.

"I'm afraid I am. MI5 anticipated this and their plan is for her to reluctantly agree to help them," explained Bill. "If she's convincing and they don't think they were detected, they'll just let her go so she can return to Bletchley and eventually get the info they want."

"So we're just going to sit back and wait? That's it?"

Bill paused, "It's all we can do. Actually, it's the plan. She won't want to blow her cover, so she won't be trying to contact us. She'll just go back to her quarters. I'll call you as soon as I know something."

Tony got undressed, tossed his clothes on the bed, put on a heavy navy blue robe and his beat up leather slippers. He took a few logs from the black iron bucket on the hearth and added them to the fireplace. The radiant heat from the glowing and crackling wood took the chill and dampness out of the room while creating a pulsating yellow glow. The stuffed chair near the fireplace beckoned again. So did the decanters of sherry and brandy on the fireplace mantle. Tony chose a full wine glass of sherry and sank into the chair. Staring intently at the dancing flames he anxiously awaited a phone call. He got up and tuned in the BBC on the radio on the mantle, put his feet up on the hassock and tried to relax. There is magic in the flicker and dancing tongues of flames, especially when accompanied by the effects of a hearty sherry. The fire and alcohol normally combined into an effective calming agent but not so easily tonight. He leaned back and tried to concentrate on the broadcast news summary of the war on both fronts. Nothing took his mind away from Petra. Tony finished off the last sips of sherry in the bottom of the glass. It tingled his tongue, imparted its characteristic woody, nutty flavor and left a warm trail down into his stomach. His troubles escaped for a while as the sherry pulled a faint veil over his eyes intermittently. He mustered up the energy to get up and walk down the hall to bed, oak boards creaking softly under his stocking feet.

Funny what dreams one's mind conjures up. Tony transitioned from dead sleep to wispy near-consciousness. His mind repeatedly wandered through visions. He was standing in the middle of a small hothouse full of golden mums, holding a small lantern, wearing only his white GI boxer shorts. The clinking of stones intermittently striking the glass panes of the hothouse had him perplexed. He turned repeatedly, trying to find the direction of the stone strikes. The darkness of night was tempered by a dull light. The puzzle of the source of the noises was progressively more frustrating. He came to full consciousness with a jolt and sat up when he realized there was tapping on his front window. He put on his slippers and went out to the living room window, peaked through the side of the blackout curtains and saw Petra's silhouette as she turned and went to the door. He quickly unlocked and opened the door, "Oh my God, I'm so glad to see you," he said as quietly as he could, "I was so worried." He closed the door and locked it behind her. "Wasn't it risky to come here? That guy could be staked out."

"Mike told me it was clear, for now, but they expect someone will show up shortly," she said. She put a small suitcase down. He looked at it wondering. "Bloody interesting night Tony; chilly one too, give us a hug, I'm shaking again. It was harrowing." They stood quietly by the door for a few moments, swaying slowly, her cheek tucked softly against his chest. Embers that lingered in the fireplace provided only a hint of light to the room. "Are you decent?" she asked with a giggle."

"Pajamas, under a robe. I'll throw a log on the fire. Brandy or sherry for the nerves?" he asked, loosening his arms and massaging her shoulders briefly.

She turned toward the fireplace, "Right! Brandy would be smashing."

"Of course," he said as he went to the fireplace and positioned logs on the embers with the stoker. She put her coat and hat on the wall hook by the door, shook out her hair with a couple tosses of her head and combed her fingers through it. One of the logs caught fire with the attendant snaps, crackles and pops, then the other one followed suit. The fire lit the room and began to cut the chill. He poured a double ration of aromatic brandy into two snifters. They touched their glasses quietly and took their first sips.

"I'm so glad that's all over," she said softly. A shiver ran through her body, nearly spilling her drink.

"I can't wait to hear the story but first I need a loo break," he said. He returned to find her sitting down cross-legged on the heavy rug in front of the fireplace with her dress tucked deep between her thighs exposing her knees.

"Oh I love the warmth of a fireplace on a cold night. The next best thing is brandy," she said as she held her palms out toward the heat. He went to the bedroom for a blanket, kneeled beside her and wrapped it around her shoulders. He then settled back on his haunches, their knees touching intermittently and picked up his glass.

"To fire and brandy," he toasted.

"Here, here!" she replied, "and thank you for the wrap." They touched their glasses again with a distinct clink and looked into each other's eyes as they sipped. "Bloody delicious, I won't ask how you managed it," she said.

"Aye, best you don't," he jested and settled onto one elbow facing her. "OK Petra, tell me. Tell me the whole thing."

She spoke softly while she stared at the dancing flames and the sparks flying from popping logs, pausing intermittently to sip brandy. He watched her eyes and facial expressions as she spoke. Each time she raised her glass, the brandy took on a deep golden glow from the fire.

"I walked directly from the bus stop toward the cinema. I had the feeling that I was being followed. I left the cinema, turned a corner and was walking along the sidewalk toward the bus stop when a car pulled alongside. A fellow in the back seat waved at me and called out that they had been looking for me and that we were late for the party, all for the benefit of passersby of course. He got out, took me by the arm firmly but careful not to appear to be forceful, whispered not to struggle or make any noise and helped me into the back seat." She paused to collect her emotions. He squeezed her hand reassuringly. "As they sped off another man in the back seat put a smelly burlap bag over my head and cuffed me hand and foot." Again she paused to fight off a shiver. "I was really worried at that point, Tony. I wasn't expecting… but, right, I got a side look at the driver though. I didn't really get much of a look at the other man in the back seat, but I jolly well got a good look at the man who grabbed me. I'm positive that I've never seen these faces before, but one thing for sure, they were Germans."

"Germans?" he blurted, trying not to speak loudly. "Sorry, continue."

"Germans, not Russians, not anything else, but bloody Germans. Their accents were excellent British but there were subtle German clues. Also, the driver got nervous and began to ask a question in German then stopped mid-sentence, realizing his mistake. The others ignored it as though nothing had been said. It certainly puts a new face on this, yes?"

"My God, this makes my head hurt. That means Kiminko or his wife is a German agent, well no, it has to be both of them. What does MI5 think about this? Never mind, go on."

"Right. Well, I'm sure MI5 will think the same thing. But identifying the Doctor remains at hand. Back to the story, they drove me around for a while convincing me that I should help them with some simple information they need. Specifically, they want a map of Bletchley Park, showing the location of all buildings their numbers and titles. I told them that I would be risking my marriage, my career and possibly being charged with treason. They reminded me that if I did not provide the map or if I told anyone about this incident, I would never see my husband or family again. Moreover they said they would kill you in front of me just before I got mine. For the kicker, they said maybe they wouldn't kill my husband, just send him photos and details about you and me. That, of course, revealed the connection with that dog's dinner swine who's been watching us at the pub. I then gave a royal command performance of fretting, hesitating and pleading, but relented and promised to make their bloody map." She turned her head from the fireplace and looked into his eyes, "I hope I convinced them. We must not do anything to make them think we'll report this. They are ruthless. They'll bloody well kill us both."

He put his empty snifter down, put his arm around her and rubbed her arm, "We'll be fine. Mike's team and MI5 are in place."

Petra sighed, "Your hands are ice cold. I hope neither of us regret getting you involved in this."

He saw the hint of something different in her eyes. "Oh don't fret about it at all, I stepped into this with my eyes open and on my own two feet. Oh, and I didn't have a choice," he laughed.

She flashed a reassuring smile, "Right. You're so different a man than I thought when I met you." Their eyes lingered for a moment then she lifted her glass to her mouth, draining the final drops of brandy.

He followed suit, then asked "When and how do you deliver the map?"

"They said they would find me in a day or two and to be prepared to give them the map straightaway. MI5 will make one they want the Germans to have, which I'll sketch a copy of and label it in my own hand."

"Of course, once you do that, they will contact you and demand something of greater intelligence value," he said.

"Quite. But they won't harm a productive source. We'll keep feeding them believable but harmless information until we have the bloody lot of them. Help us up, it's time for the love birds to do their bedroom act."

He chuckled, "And here I thought I was going to get a comfortable night's rest in my bed."

"Oh, we don't fancy the floor?" she asked with a devilish flair.

"Good for my back you know, I much prefer it," he joked.

He took her hands in his and pulled her quickly to her feet. She was unable to keep from tipping forward onto his chest. "Oops, sorry Petra, the brandy gave me extra strength."

"Likely story, Tony," she said as she pushed him back playfully. "I'm tired and don't want to sleep alone. I'm going to spend the night here if you don't mind. I brought a few things from my quarters."

"Mind? Of course not!"

Petra picked up her suitcase and went to the bedroom. She quickly undressed, pulled a night gown out of her suitcase and slipped it on, then slid into bed. "Coming to bed dear?" she called out. He came into the bedroom, turned on the light briefly while he rooted aimlessly in the armoire. Tony whispered, "Bloody cold out there on the floor once the fire burns down."

"Right. Now hush, get under this nice warm down comforter, put on our little act and go to sleep," she replied softly.

He got under the covers carefully respecting her turf. The sheets and pillow felt cold at first, but Tony's body heat, trapped by the thick down, began to warm him. He grumbled quietly, "I wish there was a fireplace in this room."

"Bloody hell, give us peace," she whispered, "mind your side and behave."

"Well, I'll try," he said. "I'm being very serious when I say I really appreciate this."

"Try bloody hard," she whispered with emphasis, "or it's back onto the floor with you."

They resumed normal voices and acted out a tryst of love birds, complete with sensual verbiage, moans, squeaking mattress springs and the subtle laughter that follows those special moments.

The act concluded and they settled in for much needed sleep. He kept to the edge of the bed, lying on his side, with his back to her. The brandy made him sleepy but at the same time her presence caused his mind to race. Petra's description of her abduction meandered through his consciousness causing him to toss and turn. She seemed also to be unable to find a comfortable position. He tucked the blanket and comforter tight under his chin. Tony's eyes became progressively heavier, despite her nearness and the effects of their love skit. Finally, he thought, I may get some rest. Petra's movements became less pronounced and farther apart. She was slipping into dreamland.

Tony awoke slowly at dawn, sunlight peeking through the sides of the blackout curtains. Suddenly his mind came into gear with the sensations of Petra tucked tight against his side, her head resting on his arm, her hand resting on his forearm. He lay still, confused, thinking he was dreaming yet he felt as though he was fully awake. Her breathing was long and deep, her body luxuriating in deep slumber. Their subconscious minds somehow during the night found the comfort two beings can share, drawing them to each other's touch. Tony was faced with a dilemma. Fake sleep and let her discover this and make her quiet retreat or to try and get up without waking her. Lying dead still, faking sleep seemed the best option.

Tony didn't have to wait long before she began to stir slightly. He regretted that this cozy situation was coming to an end. Tucked deep into a soft mattress under a couple GI blankets and a thick down comforter with her warm body alongside him was more than pleasant. Her outstretched leg began to move slowly up onto his leg. As her night gown rode up her thigh, the feel of her bare leg on his was overwhelming. Then her palm began to move slowly up and down softly over the hair on his arm. His mind raced, wondering if she was conscious of what she was doing. When her hand moved onto his chest and he felt her lips softly kissing his shoulder, he rolled toward her. "Well, good morning," he whispered.

"Good morning love," she whispered back. Their lips moved slowly together for a soft kiss.

"Is this a convincing act for the Scot? Shall I open the blackout curtains?" he asked teasingly.

"Oh no, I'm not acting," she murmured, "bloody tempting this. Being with you just makes things all tickety-boo."

"Carpe diem," he said in a low voice between kisses, "bloody tempting indeed." She rolled onto her side facing him. He began moving his hand in small circles over the smooth silk material on her back. He pulled her closer while caressing her back from her neck to the round of her buttocks. Their kisses became more hungry and animated. Tony's hand slid down over the bunched up material of her night gown onto her bare thigh. Her fingers moved down slowly over his stomach, He pulled one of the shoulder straps down over her arm exposing a breast and kissed his way down her neck and shoulder. Their passion rose rapidly and consumed them.

17 NIGHT RAID

The Mansion, Bletchley Park

Tony made his usual morning visit to his desk in the Mansion's garage loft, albeit a little later than usual. There was a note on his desk, pencil written in the impeccable long-hand of Hardcastle's Yeoman on a flimsy yellow lined quarter-page slip of paper. It said simply "Call on Captain Hardcastle at 0800 please."

He had an hour to kill. He read his daily message file and caught up on interdepartmental memos. He mused, once again, with the idea of trying to talk Hardcastle out of the loft desk arrangement, but since Hardcastle had assigned it purposely and without qualification, he came to the obvious conclusion that it was prudent not to challenge the Captain.

When he entered the Captain's office he was surprised to see Petra sitting on one of the chairs in front of the Captain's desk. She blushed slightly when their eyes met. He fought off the strong desire to smile at her. Vivid mental reruns of their wakeup a few hours earlier were battling for his conscious attention. "Good morning Captain, Second Officer Wilkinson," said Tony. "I received your message to report sir."

"Have a seat, Commander, we're waiting for a courier that should be here presently," said Hardcastle. "While we wait, I want to say that during my visit to the Operations Center in London yesterday I was given an update on what you two have been working on. I wanted to take this opportunity to tell you that I apologize for mistrusting you commander."

Tony could barely believe what he was hearing. "Thank you Captain, but no apologies are in order, sir," said Tony.

"Quite," replied Hardcastle.

Hardcastle's Yeoman received a brief phone call and departed for a few moments, then returned. "A courier arrived and said this package is for Captain Hardcastle's eyes only," she said as she set the package on the Captain's desk.

Hardcastle's eyebrows twitched nervously as he took a pocket knife from his middle desk drawer and opened the double wrapped package. "The inner wrap is addressed to you Wilkinson, from MI5," he said and handed the pen knife and package to her.

She worked diligently on the wide brown glue-backed tape on the inner wrapper. "Ah, here we go. Cover letter says that this is the map of Bletchley Park they want me to deliver to the agents." She then walked over to the fireplace on the side wall of the Captain's office, crumbled the cover letter and tossed it into the flames. "Captain, I'll need some paper and a pencil to redraw this map in my own hand sir." Hardcastle nodded and retrieved a lined pad from his desk drawer. Petra pulled a page out from the middle of the pad and went straight to work making her copy. When she finished, she rolled the copy from MI5 into a loose ball and tossed it into the fireplace. She folded her map into a size that fit into her shoulder bag.

Livingston's Lion's Pride Pub
Near Bletchley Park

The Scot ambled in a bit later than Tony, ordered a pint and took a seat at a small table across from Tony.

Petra arrived 20 minutes later. "Been here long?" she asked.

"About an hour," he said. "I wondered if I would see you tonight."

"Pint of house draft Doc," she called to the bartender as she hung her hat and coat, then took Tony's hand and dragged him from his stool to dance. It put them in earshot of The Scot, "I've got a splitting headache, I'm going to finish the pint, walk back to Bletchley to see the chemist and go home."

"I'll walk you," said Tony.

"Oh thank you love, but no worries, I'll be fine."

The Scot quickly polished off his pint and departed the pub. "Bloody hell, Mike was right, make it convenient and it will force him to act," she whispered in Tony's ear.

"Let's just hope Mike and MI5 are right about the rest of this plan," Tony whispered back.

They danced, exchanged small talk and flirted innocuously. It was the first somewhat private moments they shared since she left the cottage that morning. They wanted to hug and be close, but they were also mindful of the wisdom of not being too publicly affectionate in front of other Bletchley workers. When they had finished their pints, they bundled up and went outside.

"Hope you feel better," he said.

"Thank you, I'm sure I will, I'll see you tomorrow at work," she said. They squeezed each other's hands.

Each step of the way along the narrow winding road to his cottage, his worry deepened. His gray-gloved fists slowly clenched inside his bridge coat pockets as he reacted to the mounting tension. Were Mike and MI5 watching her close enough? Would the Germans make contact tonight? Folded in amongst all the vignettes of the German agents his mind conjured up were this morning's blissful moments with Petra. Each time her vision appeared, it put a smile on his face.

Tony locked the cottage door behind him, enjoyed a snifter of brandy by the fireplace and made his way to bed. With any luck, he would be able to fall asleep but lightly enough so that he would hear the phone if it rang.

Increasingly louder knocking sounds on the back door of the cottage eventually awakened Tony. He quietly sat up and slid his feet out from under the covers and planted them on the cold floor. He opened the drawer of the side table and took out his .45 caliber pistol. He cycled the action to bring a live round into the chamber and unlocked the gun's safety latch. The knocking repeated as he slowly walked to the door and took a position on one side of the door. "Who is it?" he asked.

"Mike," came a whispered but forceful reply. Tony mentally confirmed his distinctive voice and unlocked the door, "Mike, what the hell are you doing?"

"You can put that away for now," Mike whispered, pointing at Tony's gun, "the Germans have a man watching your front door from a distance but nobody on the back. Put some work clothes on and bring your weapon. I could use another body. I have a car waiting for us down the lane."

Tony quickly put on his boondockers, khaki shirt and trousers, foul weather jacket and watch cap. "What's going on?" asked Tony as he dressed.

"They picked her up while she was walking to a drop they gave her on the way to the base. She couldn't tell you they gave her drop instructions so that you'd act normally. Now, Bletchley just decrypted an order sent to the Doctor to detain her, maybe they smell a rat. They lost the tail we had on them but we know where they took her," said Mike.

"Holy shit!" Tony exclaimed.

"Let's hurry, time is wasting," said Mike. Tony shut and locked the back door, they squeezed through a gap in the hedge and quick-paced a half block to a black sedan. It was parked by a line of trash bins along a brick wall, puffing gray exhaust that was highlighted by the man in the moon.

Mike opened the back door of the sedan, grabbed a walkie-talkie from the seat and motioned for Tony to get in. Mike stood with one foot on the running board, extended the antenna on the walkie and radioed, "Forester this is Carpenter, over." Mike pressed the earpiece to his ear. "Roger... Roger... departing with Shoemaker, out." He folded the antenna and jumped in beside Tony. The door no sooner closed when the driver popped the clutch.

"Oh my God, this isn't good!" said Tony.

"Roger, not how we expected it to go, but we have it under control," said Mike.

"OK, where is she now? Where are we going and what am I doing?" asked Tony, adrenaline beginning to pulse through his system, his blood feeling like boiling liquid.

"By the way Tony, you're call sign is Shoemaker in case you have to use the walkie. Forester is my operations center at the embassy."

"And you are Carpenter," quipped Tony, stating the obvious.

Mike chuckled, "Yep, OK, here's what MI5 told us, when she took her map to the drop they did another grab and have taken her to a small one-story commercial building in Milton-Keynes. We're going there now. It was vacant since the war started, but about six months ago, someone rented the property, apparently a sleeper agent. It was mentioned in some illicit messages. Not directly, but MI5 put DF fixes and enough other data together to ID it. It's that second location we've been talking about."

Tony pondered all this as his mind sped through all the new information, "It's all beginning to make sense!"

"Sense or not Tony, we need to take the building before they have a chance to do her harm or do whatever they plan to do with that place. We know where everyone lives that set foot in there in the past two weeks, so while my guys take the warehouse, MI5 will fan out and arrest the others and seize their residences simultaneously."

Tony scratched his ear as his mind tumbled, "What happened to cause them to take this drastic measure? Was her cover blown?"

"Well, MI5 thinks that the Germans have gotten some intel that pushed them over from curious about the purpose of Bletchley Park to being white hot with interest. Since she's probably the first one to show any interest in giving them information, they are going for the brass ring sooner rather than later."

"I heard the Kiminkos are involved in that place. How's that being handled? asked Tony.

"I think MI5 is going to let that one unravel itself later, not sure exactly what they have in mind, unless one or both of them are in there now," said Mike.

"Alright, now, what do you want from me?" asked Tony.

"Ever get any training on the Tommy Gun?" asked Mike.

Tony chuckled, "No, just the M-1 and the .45."

"Well, you're going to get the accelerated course. I have one in the trunk for you, along with a gas mask. The gun is pretty straight forward, take off the safety, point it at something you want to damage, hold on tight and pull the trigger in short bursts. The magazine holds 30 rounds."

"OK, what's the plan?" asked Tony.

"We're going to move in on foot from a couple blocks away. There's some good cover both front and back and we should easily remain undetected. I have two men watching the back door now. You'll be the third and be sure to have your gas mask on. I'll join the guys that will rush the front door."

Mike continued rattling off information while the driver weaved through side streets toward their target. "They haven't posted any outside lookouts to date, but surveillance reports that there's probably a couple goons right inside the front office door. Neither the big garage-like door on the front or the rear door have been observed being used. The windows are all painted, so it doesn't appear that they can see outside. When the men you're with at the back door hear us attack in front, they will break in the back door and toss a tear gas grenade. Rush in after them, protect yourself, whatever it takes. Our attack begins when we toss tear gas through windows in front. The two men you're following have the sole purpose getting Petra out of there. You are going to be looking for a radio operator, guy with a walkie or telephone and take them out. We don't want them to get any word out to anyone. If you see any crypto equipment or code books, grab them and get out as soon as we clear the place, then head back to the sedan."

"What do you know about the floor plan?" asked Tony."

"As far as we can tell, there is a single open bay, about 20 by 20 feet, with a closed room, about 8 by 10 feet, that has its own door. We have no information on what they've done with it after they occupied it. OK, we're getting close now."

The driver shut off the yellow parking lights and moved very slowly through a small street as they neared the building. The bright moon provided their only visibility. The driver pulled over and shut off the lights and engine. Mike leaped out, opened the trunk and handed Tony a Thompson submachine gun, red filtered flashlight and a gas mask. After Mike gave Tony the speed course on the weapon, he said "OK, let's go find Team Baker." They moved slowly and carefully along the side of an alley that led to the warehouse. Mike held his hand over most of the flashlight lens so only a small amount of light emitted. Mike blinked a flashlight code at Team Baker and moved quietly up to them, crouched behind some wooden barrels.

They had a clear view of the rear entrance of the warehouse. A mere hint of light emitted from the bottom of the door. "This is Commander Tony Romella. You two go in first, Tony will follow you, he's looking for communicators and code books," Mike whispered to the men. They acknowledged with hand signals; Mike slapped Tony on the shoulder and disappeared into the darkness. Tony exchanged nods with the two men peering at him eerily through gas mask lenses, put on his gas mask and kneeled behind them. Minutes passed like an eternity. All the while, Tony's heartbeat and breathing accelerated. Three loud bangs in rapid succession signaled the raid was on; tear gas canisters were now spewing their acrid fog inside the building. The two men immediately bolted for the rear door. Tony was right behind them. One of the men was carrying a large heavy battering ram with a tommy gun strapped over his shoulder. The ram took the door handle and lock out in one powerful slam. They rushed into the open bay; the entry team had already taken out everyone that was in the open bay. Tony kicked opened the door to the room partitioned from the open bay. A man was standing at alert next to the chair to which Petra was lashed. The man never had a chance to do more than begin to raise his Luger pistol before Tony put several fatal shots to the man's face and chest. The two Baker team men grabbed Petra, still blindfolded, gagged and lashed to a chair and hauled her, still in the chair, out the back door into the night. Tony grabbed what he was certain was a code book on a table next to a radio set with a hand key, hurried out the back door and pulled off his mask. The sound of boots guided him until he saw their red flashlights heading for Mike's car. His eyes adjusted to the dim light of the moon, being filtered by a passing cloud, as he caught up to them. He smiled when he saw them put the chair down next to Mike's car, cut her free and remove her blindfold and gag.

"Bloody good show," she whispered, rising unsteadily from the chair, straining to see the faces of her liberators.

"Are you OK?" asked Tony.

"Oh! I am so glad to see you," she said, and threw herself in Tony's arms, "Yes, I am fine, bloody hell, as you say!" They hugged tightly. The team leader grabbed Tony's shoulder, "You remain here with her, we're going back to help with a little cleanup, won't be long before Mike will rejoin you here."

The sound of boots running Tony's way put him on alert. Tony, Petra and the driver took cover behind the car. Mike's bouncing red flashlight came into view. Tony remained cautious until the runner was close enough to recognize.

"Everyone OK?" asked Mike.

"Affirmative," said Tony. "Anyone get away?"

"Not a one. The bodies, one seriously wounded female, some documents and other evidence are being removed now and taken to our remote site for analysis. And Tony, the female is probably the good Russian Major's wife, Nastasiya. She was in the open bay, unconscious but still alive, so we're taking her to a location MI5 told us to take any survivors."

"Major wasn't there?"

"Negative, and that could be a real problem. If he was privy to it all, then he probably won't make a peep. He can't reveal their involvement with a German spy cell. God only knows how he'll react, and holy hell, he has to explain her absence. Oh I damn sure don't envy him. Their NKGB Rezidentura will rain hell on his parade if he finds out what they're up to."

"How about the Scot?"

Mike shrugged, "Not there either, so that end of the fire hose is still loose and flapping around. I have people on him, they may already have him in custody. Where to Tony? Petra?"

"My London flat, not that I'll be able to get any sleep with all this adrenalin," said Tony.

"Saint James Street if you please," said Petra, "I've got some work to do at the office before I sleep."

U.S. Naval Attaché Office
London

"Good morning! Well, that was quite a night for you all!" said Captain Taylor as he entered the conference room. Tony, Petra and Mike all returned greetings and displayed smiles as the Captain took his chair. "OK Mike, update."

"Captain, things are suspiciously quiet. Major Kiminko remains at the estate and no vehicles have left there since his wife departed for the warehouse last night. The Scot is ridiculously cagey, we just haven't been able to isolate his home plate. An MI5 agent was dispatched about 20 minutes ago to join up with our team assigned to find the damn guy. We're checking all the places we've seen him at before. We will find him and bring him in. I'll keep you posted."

Captain Taylor nodded, "Any preliminary intelligence from the documents?"

Mike shifted in his chair, "I have nothing on that yet. It's too soon, but everything was taken promptly to Site Oscar where analysts have been cataloging and translating all night. We should have the first reports later today. There was quite a bit to sort through. There were about 30 bombs, some pretty damn large. Also quite a bit of bomb making materials. Not sure yet what the targets were going to be. I'll let you all know as soon as I get some results of the analysis and documents."

Bill Taylor turned to Petra and lifted his jaw slightly.

"Right," she said acknowledging her turn, "Sorry to say, Nastasiya never regained consciousness and succumbed to her wounds last hour. Bletchley reports nothing heard on the short-wave from the Doctor since night before last, which is bloody frustrating, but good at the same time. Nothing has been heard from the Russian embassy, no protests, no masked condemnations, no apparent recall of the Major to Moscow, nothing. Our DG briefed Churchill and a few of his senior staff." She turned to Tony.

"Well, well," said Tony, "this will be interesting. If the Doctor transmits again, it probably means it's the Major. Unless, of course, we can account for his presence at a location and time that contradicts that assumption."

Mike smiled, "There's a possibility that the Doctor is more than one person, perhaps even a duty radio operator that has no idea what he's sending or to whom."

Tony shook his head, "No, the Doctor's fist on the key is unique. The Russian radio operators sending normal short-wave messages from their embassy to Moscow appear to be three different radio operators on rotating shifts. I have listened to them so I know firsthand. What's more, the Kiminkos would not in any way be able to trust such unusual transmissions to an embassy radio operator. They are in a precarious position and can't risk anyone wondering about or questioning their actions in the embassy."

"Fist?" asked Mike.

"Yes, fist being a term for the subtle characteristics of the speed, spacing, swing, duration and finite characteristics of dots and dashes. You can reliably identify a manual Morse operator, it's like a fingerprint. No two are exactly the same. Agent transmissions are normally done by hand and by the agent personally. I would discount the idea of a second party. So, with the Scot still on the loose, things have changed in some respects. He may or may not know about the warehouse raid. He may have a different set of tasks, or is trying to escape from the U.K. by some covert process that escapes our surveillance. He doesn't necessarily have to drive out that front gate, for example." Everyone was nodding. "What's our best plan of action now?"

Petra took a deep breath, "We watch everything, listen for the Doctor, see what develops from interrogations and documents and best of all, you and I are bait again Tony. Bill and I had a discussion about this a little while ago. Sorry I didn't have time to confer with you and Mike first, but there hasn't been time," she said.

Bill nodded, "I recall you like fly fishing, right Tony?"

Tony laughed, "Yes, I sure do, but I'm more accustomed to being on the other end of the line. OK, what is it this time?"

Bill chuckled then took on a serious look, "Tony, a lot of things have been going on before this meeting. As you heard, MI5 and Mike's teams have been authorized to capture the Scot dead or alive. So, if he isn't aware of what happened last night and we're pretty sure he isn't since Kiminko hasn't left the estate, in order to draw him out, you're going back to Bletchley on Monday. Petra's going back this afternoon."

Petra injected, "Right, we're pretty sure he's close to making contact with one of us, and it's more likely me than you, Tony. So, we carry on, and make it both convincing and easy for him to make his move."

"But Tony," the Captain interrupted, "you have a weekend commitment. I received an invitation to a reception at Lady Watson's for Saturday evening and some horseplay Sunday morning. I am flying to Dublin tomorrow and doubt I'll be back in time. Kiminko and other attachés are also invited. It will be interesting to find out if the good Major shows up and if so, how he acts."

18 ASYLUM

Havenwood--Estate of Lady Inga Watson
Suburb of London

Inga was standing just inside the receiving room door off the foyer where the formal reception of London attachés and other prominent personalities was underway. Tony was next to be greeted behind a man in a tuxedo and his lady. They were being properly fussed over by Inga. Tony took advantage of the opportunity to admire Inga's mint green gown and cleavage without much risk of being caught while she was preoccupied.

"Commander, so nice to see you again. Did Captain Taylor come with you?" she asked when he became next in line.

Tony smiled as he approached and took her hand, "He sends his regrets and sent me to represent him."

"I am disappointed he can't be here but delighted that you could. Don't we look just smashing," she said playfully inspecting him from head to toe, "Please make yourself comfortable and enjoy some refreshments," she said with that magic twinkle in her eye and velvet voice. Tony couldn't help but be amused by Inga, a lady of very obvious high intelligence, status and resources but yet so human and intriguing. He quickly scanned the room as he walked toward one of the two bars along the rear wall. The Russian Major was nowhere among the many different uniforms interspersed with tuxedos and fine gowns. Those present were mingling, huddling in small groups and helping themselves to a tempting array of hors d'oeuvres arrayed on long tables on either side of the bar. He kept his eye on the door for the Major all the while wandering the room, sampling the food, nursing a splendid 12 year old scotch and exchanging small talk with the attendees.

Tony felt butterflies take flight in his gut as he looked up from the caviar table to see Major Kiminko being welcomed by Inga. He rapidly thought through possible scenarios. He planned his reactions and behavior for each of them. He decided to let the Major come to him, so he continued his random mingling. It seemed as though the Major was totally disinterested in Tony and managed to remain distant as they both moved about the room. Tony glanced aside as he picked up a soda cracker adorned artfully with a pâté and noticed the uniform pants next to him were the Major's. Tony looked up casually and feigned surprise, "Well, good evening Major, nice to see you again."

"Good evening Lieutenant Commander, how was your week?" asked Kiminko, as he offered up his glass to touch against Tony's.

"It was quite good. How have you been sir?"

The Major seemed to stumble in thought for a brief moment, then said, "Well, life has many surprises, but for that my parents warned me. Such is normal for a soldier, da? Tell me, your assignment in London, are you still enjoying?"

"It has its moments," Tony said with a sly grin, "but we press on."

Their eyes were locked as each pair penetrated deep into the other, seeking what may be in hiding behind the retinas in the gray matter. Kiminko broke the uncomfortable moments, "Da, we press on comrade. Do you get out of London to see the countryside Commander?"

"Not really, I haven't had a chance to take leave and travel on my own."

"Ah, leave, as you call it, is for me a rare occasion. The war makes it impossible. The last leave I had was three years ago, in Baku," said Kiminko, who paused and failed to finish the rest of the sentence.

Tony detected the slightest hint of emotion in Kiminko's eyes and decided to push a little on the Major, "Perhaps one day I'll get to visit the Caspian Sea. Did you vacation there with your wife? By the way, I notice that she isn't here. Sorry she was unable to be here tonight. She is well I trust?"

Kiminko's dark brown eyes peered out from under bushy gray eye brows and began shifting his shoulders as his face flushed, "Nastasiya had," he stammered, "other commitments." He was clearly irritated and searching for words as his eyes again bored into Tony's.

"We all seem to be overextended these days, the pressures of the war are tremendous. It must be troubling that your homeland is being threatened by the German army," said Tony.

"Da Commander," Kiminko replied and looked away.

Tony extended his hand, "Major, a pleasure. My glass is empty and I need to say hello to some of the others."

Kiminko shook hands with a strong grip which lingered perceptibly while he searched for some words, "I might ask a favor of you sometime Commander, perhaps a small trade of harmless information."

"One can always ask Major," said Tony with a jesting tone.

The Major did not smile. "Sometimes Commander, we seek information that cannot be handled through normal channels, da?" Tony nodded while he considered a proper response and pondered how to handle the developing conversation. The Major continued, "How might I contact you Commander for such a request, with uh, discretion?"

"I expect to be attending Lady Watson's receptions," said Tony.

Kiminko nodded, "But if I want to speak with you before that or elsewhere?"

Tony nodded, "Call this number and ask for me. If I am not in, they will take a message and I will return the call as soon as I can," said Tony as he jotted a special number for the Attaché office on one of his calling cards. "Do you have a number where you can be reached Major?"

Kiminko paused, his eyes looking away for a moment, "No, but if you get a call from me, regardless what I say to you or the message I leave, it means we meet in Regent's Park at 10 pm that night. Walk through York gate, then turn left on the inner circling walk path around Queen Mary's garden. You will see benches by the lake. There will be no need to contact me or return the call. It is important that you do not try to call me."

Tony noted in the Major's eyes and body language that the Major had given this forethought and was experiencing a degree of fear. He clearly was putting himself at risk. "I understand Major and will respect your need for discretion. Is there something I can do to prepare for this request? What is the general topic?"

The Major responded rapidly and forcefully, "I cannot say that. Just wait for my call." Kiminko smiled, more for show than anything else, shook Tony's hand again and walked to the bar.

Following Monday
U.S. Naval Attaché Office
London

Tony gave Bill and Mike a detailed account of the conversation he had with Major Kiminko. Bill pulled close to the conference table when Tony finished, "I have to say, you handled that really well Tony, but you took a big chance agreeing to meet and exchange information. MI5 may have a royal fit over this. I called Petra, caught her just as she was getting ready to leave for Bletchley. She's on her way over here, due in ten minutes or so. But I wanted the three of us to meet first."

Tony stood up, "Damn it, I didn't feel like I had a choice, it didn't seem prudent to pass on the opportunity and I knew Mike could handle the security issues. We've had a hell of a time finding the Scot. It seemed to me it was a way of possibly getting a hint at what's going on inside their little operation. Sorry, I just feel strongly about this." He sat down.

They sat quiet for a few moments. Mike broke the silence, "MI5 might be pissed off, maybe not. Actually, although it was a gutsy move and it would have been better if we had anticipated it and provided guidance to Tony beforehand, I can't really see a negative side to it."

Bill shook his head, "I don't give a rat's ass what we see and or feel about it, I just hate the idea that we may well have overstepped our relationship with MI5."

They paused their conversation while a Seaman brought in a tray of scones, a pot of coffee and a handful of mugs.

"Go ahead and dig in while we're waiting for Petra," said Bill.

"Sorry it took longer than expected, I had to make another stop," said Petra as she helped herself to a scone and mug of coffee. "I don't normally drink coffee, but I fancy something hot, yes?"

"Petra, we have some good news and some bad news," Bill said.

"OK, give us the good news first, then I'll tell you my news," she said.

"Well the good news and bad news is all run together," said Bill, "In a nutshell, at the reception last night at Havenwood, Tony was approached by Major Kiminko to meet outside of channels for an exchange of information, not specified. Give her the details." Bill nodded at Tony.

Tony repeated his experience with Major Kiminko. He became aware of a grin forming on her face as he related the story. She took a sip of coffee to wash down a bite of scone and said, "They called me to the office to tell me that the Doctor transmitted a report last night about the missing personnel and the compromise of the building they were operating from. Kiminko just has to be the Doctor."

Bill felt relief that she was not reflecting any objection to the situation that developed with the Major. "Given all you know right now Petra, is there any hint of what Kiminko will be asking for?" asked Bill.

"No, that's a mystery. What's your sense of it?" she asked.

Bill and Tony shrugged, but Mike had a contribution, "Well, I see it one of several ways. He could be looking for asylum, he could be looking for information on Nastasiya and the others, or maybe he even wants to negotiate a return or trade. I hope we're keeping the bodies on ice. We may need them."

Petra nodded, "Quite. But he has nothing to trade unless he gives up the Scot and any other hooligans still milling about."

Captain Taylor shook his head, "He can't do that, he'd be compromising his entire covert operation, risk having them all being decertified by the Brits. At the very least, that would be a diplomatic scandal at the highest level. Moscow damn sure wouldn't think much of that. Kiminko would be a dead man and he doesn't strike me as having a death wish.

"Makes asylum looking more like the objective then doesn't it?" asked Tony. Bill and Petra shrugged. There was a sullen look on Mike's face, "What are you thinking?" asked Tony.

"Well, I think there's another possibility. He can grab you so he has something to trade for safe passage," said Mike. "You've both been targets of the Scot. We better make damn sure we have constant protective coverage on both Petra and Tony. If I was the Major, I'd rethink the risk of meeting at Regent's Park. It should be obvious to him that we'd be prepared."

Petra nodded, "Spot on. It will be interesting to see what their next move is going to be. Bloody hell, let's put together a good plan for Regent's Park."

Regent's Park
London

Major Kiminko made his cryptic call to the Naval Attaché Office two days later. The message was simply "Please thank Commander Romella for the brandy, it was a rare treat." Bill notified Tony, Petra and Mike, setting in motion the plan they developed a few days earlier. As soon as darkness descended upon the park, MI5 agents and Mike's team covertly took up their stations at various locations in the park. MI5 had been observing the park continuously for two days. To the best of their knowledge, no one of suspicion was in the park at the moment. At 9:30 PM Tony departed the embassy alone in a black embassy coupe. He felt excitement building as he turned off the A501 at the first exit for the park's Outer Circle road and then found the turn onto York Bridge road. At the intersection of the Inner Circle, he pulled to the side and turned off the engine. He got out of the car, partially closed the door and walked slowly along the inner circle. A sliver of moon, filtered through humid haze, provided just enough light to see. The weight of a .45 caliber pistol tucked in a shoulder holster was comforting although he was painfully alert. There was no place for MI5 and Mike's agents to hide close to the open area of the inner circle. He knew he was essentially on his own if Kiminko made a quick aggressive move. But all points of egress were covered, so there was no escape. The air was damp and crisp but just the same he had his dress blue uniform jacket unbuttoned and the top buttons of his bridge coat unbuttoned for easy access to the pistol. He carried gray gloves in his left hand. He adjusted his white silk scarf to better block the bite of the cold on his neck. Eerie quiet was broken intermittently by the hoot of an owl which he envied for being better able to see his surroundings. He stopped by the first park bench he came to and slowly turned about looking for movement, then sat down. Ten minutes passed before Tony heard subtle noises to his left of ground crunching softly under someone's shoes. In a few moments he saw the outline of a man approaching. Tony's heart began to beat stronger and more quickly; he kept the shape in focus and stood. The silhouette of a Russian officer's hat was unmistakable. "Good evening Major."

Kiminko stopped a few feet in front of Tony, "Good evening Commander," the Major replied curtly, his hands still in his coat pockets. It was clear this was not going to be a meeting with a lengthy exchange of pleasantries. The Major continued, "You have kept your word Commander, as have I, we are alone, da?."

"Indeed Major," said Tony.

They looked into each other's dark and featureless faces for a few moments before Kiminko spoke again, "Let me speak with frankly Commander. I am wanting to see my wife, Nastasiya. Can you arrange a secret meeting?"

Tony's heart was pounding. He mulled over a response. "This is a difficult question, Major," he said, hoping a delay in responding would allow just the right words to float into his consciousness.

"Da, I offer nothing to you but ask for something again, no?" asked the Major.

"Exactly Major but there are complications," said Tony.

"Da? Tell me."

"Let me ask you a question Major, which of you is in charge of the German espionage operations, you or Nastasiya?" Tony surprised himself, wandering where that question came from.

"Commander, it is the job of the attaché office to collect intelligence, no?

Tony was puzzled by the attempted diversion, "Major, no games. We agreed. I'm speaking of espionage, not intelligence. Your organization has been conducting very secret operations, including assassinations. Your wife claims that she does not know the names and locations of all the agents involved with these operations. She knows that these operations are taking place, but does not give us the details we seek. It must be you Major who has these details." Tony's imagination to use this line was intended to shock the Major. And shock it did. Kiminko stood like one of the stone statues in Red Square for what seemed like minutes. The only evidence of life in his body was the frosty puffs of breath from his nostrils visible in the faint moonlight. Tony wished he could see the Major's surprised expression. "You need not say anything Major, your silence is an answer," said Tony. "Perhaps Major, this would be a good time to make a change in your life and career. Moscow will not be happy with you if it learns you are a German agent. You know that MI5 discovered your secret building and captured your wife and some of your agents. And Major, my guess is that Nastasiya's disappearance has alarmed the NKGB and that you have been, or soon will be, invited to return to Moscow." Tony paused to see if Kiminko would interject. There was nothing but silence. "You and I both know Major, that your life as a traitor to Russia will come to a brutal end shortly after arriving in Moscow. There will be no hero's welcome, no debriefing or reassignment. You'll be lucky to get a funeral. Tell me you wish political asylum in the United States, get in my car and live out your normal life in a safe location in the greatest country in the world."

"And Nastasiya?" Kiminko asked.

Tony quickly mulled over the words that would neither be a lie nor complete truth. "Nastasiya will be granted the same respect we grant you and can accompany you to the United States."

"Commander, I must have time to think," said Kiminko with the voice of a shaken and beaten man.

"No Major, your ambassador and rezidentura will not give you time. You do not have any time. The decision is yours and now is the time. But I will give you five minutes before I get in my car, either with you, or without you."

"And the price of this asylum? You will put me in prison in America, dah?" asked the Major.

"No prison, freedom, with our protection from your NKGB. Your price to save your life, is to simply provide us full and complete information of all intelligence and espionage operations you have knowledge of, past, present and future. Here and worldwide, everything you know, everything!"

"Comrade," muttered Kiminko without finishing his thought. Tony observed the frosty plume of a long, deep sigh from Kiminko as he pondered his predicament and measured his words. The once proud and stoic Soviet Major whispered, "I believe your saying goes, I am painted into a corner. If I request asylum, will I see my wife immediately?"

The darkness of night hid the crimson edges of Tony's ears and flushed face. Now it was Tony who was taking time to formulate a proper response. "Major, I can only tell you that you and your wife will be treated with the respect due both of you, given your individual situations and satisfaction of the intelligence cooperation expectations of the United States and the United Kingdom."

"I want asylum in the United States for me and my wife, not the U.K. Commander, can you promise that?"

"Yes I can Major."

After an audible swallow, Kiminko snapped his heels together, saluted Tony and exclaimed with a detectable tremble in his voice, "Major Grischa Kiminko, Soviet Army is requesting political asylum in the United States. I will now surrender my weapon." Tony watched at full alert as Kiminko very slowly pulled a pistol from his overcoat, turned it slowly and carefully, grasped it by its barrel and handed it to Tony.

19 CULMINATION

Camp 020z
Northwest of London

Tony parked his jeep in front of a bomb and fire gutted building on the narrow street across from the address hand written on a card with the words Camp 020z, the classified title for an MI5 operations building. He maneuvered his two right wheels up on the curb as all others had along the street. He approached the doorway marked only by a wooden plate with the building number above the door. To the right side of the door was a temporary placard on which was printed TO LET. It was so unobtrusive, he double checked the address with the card in his pocket. He knocked three times. Shortly the door was opened by a woman in civilian clothes, "Are you here to inquire about the let sir?"

"Yes, I am Lieutenant Commander Anthony Romella, U.S. Navy," he said offering his military ID card.

"She glanced at his ID without a word and nodded as though recognizing his name, motioned him in and closed the door behind her. She took him into the first small room to the left on a long hallway. Inside the room were two Royal Army sentries armed with bayoneted rifles standing to each side of a small hardwood standup desk. One stepped forward authoritatively and asked for ID, which Tony provided. The sentry scanned a list on the desk and returned Tony's ID. A phone call was made by the sentry announcing Tony's arrival, followed by a motion for Tony to follow the woman.

This was a building commandeered by MI5 shortly into the war, located about 25 kilometers northwest of London. It was formerly a bank, now it was MI5's Camp 020z, or twenty zed as the Brits called it. This was one of a few highly classified facilities that were refurbished and outfitted specifically for handling captured spies and espionage suspects. MI5's early and continued success in identifying and capturing espionage agents made it necessary to establish secure complexes to retain and process them. Inside this building were controlled access quarters, jail cells, interrogation rooms, some offices, a comprehensive medical facility and a morgue.

Tony followed her down the hall to an elevator. "Go to B1 sir, someone will meet you there."

When the elevator doors opened, Petra was waiting with a grin. He greeted her with a return smile, "Top of the morning to you Petra, get any sleep?"

"No more than you I'm sure, bloody hell," she said. "I hope it goes well this morning with Kiminko. He's been belligerent about being held by us, not being free to leave his quarters and not getting to see his wife right away." She stopped and motioned for him to enter a room.

"Mornin' Tony," said Bill, "Mike will be here shortly and asked us to wait for him."

Petra smiled, "Right. Make yourself at home Tony, we'll have some tea and biscuits coming up soon from the kitchen. By the by, I've been replaced permanently at Bletchley, too much going on here. And we accomplished what we set out to do for the time being," she said. "Have you been pulled out as well?" she asked Tony.

He shook his head, "No, that's not the plan at this point anyway."

"Tony, before you sit, I'd like to huddle with you in the hallway a minute." When the door closed behind them, Bill put his hand on Tony's shoulder and began speaking in a soft voice, "There's been a significant development of interest to you." began Bill, "Just before I left to come over here, the OPCEN reported some Most Secret intel to me. They have corroborated intelligence, from both the French Resistance and deciphered messages, that Admiral Dönitz was apparently shaken by the success of Operation Chariot. Saint-Nazaire is just up the coast from his headquarters in Kernevel, you know. Well, he's moving his command back to Paris immediately. There will be more details as the intel comes in, but the Germans are in a rush to relocate. They have officers in the process of obtaining a suitable building in Paris, today actually. The building he was using in Paris when he moved to Kernevel is not available to him so they are scrambling to find another place suitable to the Admiral. MI6 is working on getting someone into Paris that can focus on collecting HUMINT on the Admiral and his staff. Can you believe that?"

Tony shook his head, "That had to be one tough damn decision for Dönitz to make, he clearly wanted to be close to those U-boats he commands. He must really feel vulnerable in Kernevel now. This could be really bad news for us. Here's why. Dönitz is using an HF band, short wave, encrypted teletype comm link between Kernevel and Berlin that we're reading almost as soon as Dönitz does. That might change to a telephone line circuit between Paris and Berlin and we'd lose all that intel, especially the stuff about targeting our shipping to Britain and his wolfpacks in general. That link has been especially invaluable since Dönitz implemented the 4-wheel Enigma machine for the U-boat forces on the 1st of the month. Hopefully, they'll keep that link going to support the U-boat operations there, but the level of information won't be same."

Bill nodded, "Are you saying that the source of ULTRA intel on U-boats dried up for Bletchley? Didn't you tell me they were able to determine the design impact of the 4th wheel thanks to some German U-boat operator's compromise?

"Yes I am telling you that and yes I did. Bletchley found a way to use the existing Bombe machines to decrypt the 4-wheel Enigma messages. However, it takes 26 times longer to decipher the SHARK messages that way…"

"Well what's the issue then?" Bill interrupted.

"Unfortunately, there's a catch and a damn significant one. Bear with me a moment, I'll explain. The Germans also changed their Naval Meteorological Code, which is critical for the decryption process. The U-boats use the weather code book to shorten their encrypted messages. It's a security thing, shorter air time to transmit, so less vulnerability to detection, intercept and location. The repetitive and proforma nature of the 3-digit weather code groups is a crib, or insight, into the plain text of their encrypted message. We have the old version of the met code, we don't have the new one. Without those cribs, for several days now, since they implemented SHARK on the 1st, they have not been able to read the 4-wheel Enigma traffic."

"Oh good grief, that means we don't have the wolfpack locations and thus we can't provide safe routes for the convoys. Damn Tony! We're going to start seeing a spike in convoy sinkings."

"Exactly Bill. That is why the high command link between Berlin and Dönitz is so critical. It gives us some intel, but not all we need. So, boss, we need to push for a high priority HUMINT tasking requirement to obtain the 1942 meteorological code book, or the Enigma daily setup keys, well both for that matter."

Bill nodded at Tony, "OK, so, uh, aside from HUMINT, any ideas?"

Tony smiled, "Capture a U-boat and recover the Enigma keys and met code. That's easier said than done. HUMINT is going to be the least detectable means of recovery and has the potential for ongoing, long term intel.

"Noted! Are you volunteering? Have a thirst for French wine and cheese? Bill asked with a broad grin.

"Now Bill, you and I know that's a really big damn stretch of my training and experience. Not to mention that I don't speak German or French. You're kidding I hope."

Bill laughed and slapped Tony's shoulder, "I'll get on that tasking request to DC independently of the Brits but at the same time, I'll bring it up with MI6. I'll keep you posted. OK, get back in there, I'm going down the hall to the head, be right there."

Tony took a middle seat next to Petra at the eight-place mahogany conference table.

They were alone in the conference room. She uncrossed her legs and leaned toward him. "I'll bloody miss you Tony," she whispered. "You'll get back to London, yes?"

"I'll make a point of it. It will be damn lonely without you," he whispered back. He reached down, squeezed her hand and leaned in to kiss her. They quickly retreated to neutral positions at the sound of footsteps coming toward the door.

The conference door opened, "Good morning folks," greeted Mike. Right behind him was Captain Taylor and one of the kitchen staff wearing a white bonnet and a starched white apron over a black dress. She was carrying a tray containing a tea service, a plate of biscuits and scones as well as a jar of blackberry jam with a small silver spoon with an intricate handle standing at attention in it.

"Help yourselves to the refreshments then we'll get started," said Petra.

"It's been a busy and productive couple days, yes?"

The men nodded, being polite to not attempt speaking with full mouths. Mike swallowed, "Before we get going, I got a call just before I left, one of my teams reported that they and an MI5 agent picked up the Scot in Woburn."

"Bloody good job Mike, that should wrap this little band of merry men up quite nicely," Petra said. "We'll offer him the same lovely deal we've offered the others, be a double-agent for us or be hanged in Wadsworth prison."

Tony laughed, "Anyone ever choose the Wadsworth option?"

She nodded, "Several, believe it or not. They were rotten to the core, so loyal that they just couldn't bring themselves to work with us. But, out of the lot of spies we've caught so far, all but three out of 15 actually decided not to stretch their necks and work for us instead. Nearly all of them were rounded up before or just after we declared war."

"I had no idea they could get that many agents in here," said Bill, "no wonder you're all so busy. And thank you for the refreshments Petra, I only had time for a very brief breakfast before I left my quarters."

"Quite. Now then, let's review our plan for today's unpleasant task," said Petra. "Mike and one of our interrogators worked on Kiminko extensively. They spent most of the night with him. The more tired and frustrated he got, the better the information became, but he's clearly holding back now," she laughed briefly and turned to Mike.

"Yeah, he has clammed up until he gets to talk with Nastasiya and Tony," said Mike. "They had to suspend the interrogation. They didn't have any idea how we wanted to handle telling him the about Nastasiya, so they just said they had no info on when he'd be able to see her but would get Tony in to see him ASAP."

"Why me, I wonder? Well, I guess that's rather obvious," said Tony.

"Indeed. He's complaining that he requested asylum in the United States from you and has not seen an American since he got here. Mike was not identified by nationality, just a pseudonym, so the major had no real way of knowing, aside from accent," explained Petra.

"OK, that makes sense," said Tony with a nod.

"So, let's come up with a plan to solve the two issues we have, getting more information out of him and of course, Nastasiya," said Petra.

Tony nodded at the two Royal Army guards outside the door to the Major's small suite and entered. The building had two restricted access holding suites for cooperative higher level captives in the basement, two floors below ground level. The Major was sitting at a small table in what passed for a kitchen. The suite had three other rooms: a small bedroom, full bathroom and a sitting room, all with austere décor and furnishings. "Good morning!" exclaimed Kiminko who came promptly to his feet and extended his hand for a vigorous shake. His eyes were bloodshot and he looked haggard, "Finally I speak with an American."

"Good morning Major, may I call you Grischa?" asked Tony.

"Of course, of course, I call you Tony?"

"Please do Grischa. Let's sit and discuss a few items."

They sat on opposite ends of a couch. Tony could feel the contour of springs through the brown burlap-like covering. "Better than a field tent, no Grischa?"

"Da, I don't complain."

"I have a wire recorder here, which I'll turn on in a moment, Grischa. I just want to properly document your request for asylum in the United States and our agreements. Some of my questions may possibly duplicate what you were already asked, but this is for the United States asylum documentation." Tony paused for acknowledgement from Kiminko, who nodded with a quizzical look.

Tony turned on the recorder and sat it on the cushion between them. The Major went through the formality of stating his name, rank, service, country, serial number, age and place of birth, as well as his verbal and written request for asylum in the United States. "Now Grischa, is it your desire that Nastasiya not be returned to the Soviet Union and also be granted passage to the United States?"

"Da. That is my request Tony and also to see and speak with her as soon as possible. I want to be sure she requests same things and for her to know I am cooperating full and want her to also. I don't want her to hold pride and be hanged."

"OK Grischa, the debriefing team that spoke with you previously said they have not finished and have many more questions to ask you. You may not have known it, but one of the Russian speaking interrogators was a United States representative, so we won't need to put you through all of his questions again. We just have more questions for you. So before we go further, I need your agreement to continue speaking with them so the United States gets evidence of your sincerity and valuable information in return for your asylum, OK?

"Da Tony. I will do that. I told them I would after I see my wife. Can you tell me where in the U.S. you will send me and Nastasiya?"

"The State of Virginia, near Washington, DC, then, after debriefing you thoroughly, we'll move you somewhere deeper inside the United States with new identities," said Tony.

"When?" asked Kiminko.

"We've just begun arranging safe transportation, so I don't know when yet. In the meantime, the interrogators are very interested in some of the information you have provided. It has created new questions as I mentioned. So, they want more time with you to explore some things."

Kiminko nodded, "That is good, but not until I talk with Nastasiya, that's very important for me. I must tell her of our plans. Is she here in this building?"

Tony realized he had come to a tough point in the conversation. He discussed the approach for this moment with the others upstairs extensively. Tony reached down and turned off the recorder. "Grischa, the recorder is turned off so I can talk honestly and privately between the two of us. Now, you are fully aware that the raid on your secret operations building near Milton-Keynes was not without bloodshed, correct?"

"Yes, I can expect that," he said as he took in a deep breath and tucked his hands under his arms. "Can you tell me what happened to my agents?" asked Kiminko.

"All the men in the building were killed in the raid. Nastasiya was brought directly to the surgery in this facility clinging to life, but did not survive her chest wound. She passed away the next day. They did everything they could to save her."

Grischa's faced drained and became pale as ash. His jaw clenched. His eyes began tearing profusely. His fists began pounding his thighs in a slow rhythm, harder with each strike and his breathing became heavy and rapid. Tony was prepared to stand and defend himself from a raging Russian bear. He didn't know what would follow but he was ready for anything. Kiminko's body stiffened, arched backward almost violently, then folded fully downward with his hands on his knees. His torso bounced as he cried into his hands for a moment.

"I'm so sorry to tell you this Grischa. The orders were to capture her alive. The autopsy revealed that she had taken a bullet to the chest from one of your agents that was spraying automatic weapon fire. I'm so sorry Grischa."

When Kiminko managed to bring himself into some semblance of control he said, "You say she is here in this building? I want to see her. Now Tony!"

Tony and the Major entered the markedly quiet morgue. There was a faint odor of formaldehyde. The gray painted concrete floor and clean white walls crisply echoed the door's closing and their footsteps. A physician wearing a long white coat and surgical cap introduced himself, offered his condolences and ushered them to one side of a refrigerator door in a bank of six in the wall. Tony looked at Kiminko, "Ready?"

The major took a deep halting breath and softly uttered, "Da."

The physician put on heavy canvas gloves, pulled the stainless steel lever on the door labeled 4 and opened it wide. Smokey fumes billowed out and faded away as though dry ice was being exposed. The sight of the contour of her body under a white sheet caused the major to lose his composure.

The physician put his hand up to prevent the major from moving closer, "First, Major, I want to warn you, don't touch the body or the stainless steel slide mechanism underneath. They are at minus 40 degrees centigrade, which will damage your skin on contact. This procedure was used because we don't know how long it will be before her transportation to the United States is arranged or by what means." Kiminko, sullen and pensive, managed a shaking nod. The physician pulled on a hand grip at the end of the stainless steel tray containing the remains and slid the tray out fully. The physician then slowly pulled the upper end of the sheet down to reveal Nastasiya's head and shoulders. Kiminko stared down at her in disbelief. A bullet hole was clearly visible in her chest several inches below her left clavicle. Kiminko began shaking and turned briefly away from the others. He returned his gaze to her face and instinctively began to move his hand toward her head but pulled back when Tony motioned to block his hand. The Major sobbed and spoke to her in Russian for several minutes. Kiminko became quiet for a few moments, then whispered a few final words to her. He turned and looked at physician, "Take good care of Nastasiya, doctor."

Tony took Kiminko back to his suite and went in search of some vodka. Returning with the closest thing he could find, a bottle of gin, he poured some into juice glasses. Handing one to the major, Tony raised his glass and toasted in poor Russian, "nastrovia, to better times Grischa."

The major managed a slight semblance of a grin, "na zdrowie Tony, we can hope for better." Kiminko downed it, walked to the couch and slumped into it

Tony noted that Mike's wire recorder had been removed when he sat on the other end of the couch. "Grischa, I'm curious, I'm sorry if you've already been asked, but, how did you and Nastasiya meet?"

The major smiled, "Spy equipment school in Moscow. She was NKGB, intelligence department. When they found out we were liking each other, they let us marry. Being the wife of a GRU officer, doing military attaché duty, would be good cover for her."

Tony nodded, "Yes I can see that would be useful. How in hell did you wind up spying for the Germans?

Kiminko stared into his empty glass for a moment, "Oh, a long story Tony. Short one, they caught Nastasiya on a secret mission in Berlin, you call it taps. Uh, she was putting taps on phone lines of a German General's house. I was assigned to our embassy in Amsterdam then. They gave her choice, they kill us both, or both of us spy for Germany. And if we don't spy for them, they also kill our two children, our mothers and fathers too. So, we spy. We try not to give all they want, but they are smart and dangerous. Our son and daughter have professions and families. So, we keep spying. A circle, da?"

"Indeed! I can't imagine having to make such a decision. I hope I never have to make one anything like that. Grischa, I'm not recording or writing any of this down, I'm just curious. We've come to know each other and I am so surprised by all of this."

"Not surprised as me, Tony. Now I have to worry about my children and families. Can you make it so we just disappear? Or both killed so Germans don't care about us or families?"

Tony's penchant for promptly making logical decisions kicked in, sometimes before paving the way through bureaucracy, "We will report to Moscow that you both were killed and cremated due our lack of body storage. We'll provide some ashes. We will contact our Embassy in Moscow and ask them to try to get your children and their kids out of there. No promises that we can do that for them of course."

Kiminko smiled broadly, "I like that plan Tony," as he pointed at the bottle of gin.

Tony poured each of them a hearty ration. They each took a big sip. "Now Grischa, here in London, what was the mission the Germans gave you?"

"All normal military intelligence Tony, you know, air bases, naval bases, Ministry of Defense, whatever we learn. But they are special interested about Bletchley Park, we found out it was the school for code machine operators. It was a place we can learn how code equipment works." Kiminko smiled, "And your affair with Petra, a married woman, made her someone to bring information. I am sorry for that, Tony. You would do same, da?"

"I'm sure I would. So, the warehouse, what was going on there? You may as well tell me, they are learning about all the things they took out of there, but, like I say, I'm curious and can't wait to find out."

Kiminko shook his head and polished off his gin, "You ask questions in different way, but is OK. That mission I didn't like, I think it was too dangerous, MI5 is too good, but the Germans don't listen. We make bombs, for buildings in ports getting shipping from America. They haven't said the ports or buildings yet. Just we make bombs and report number finished each week."

"Who was the radio operator Grischa? I assume that's how you reported to Berlin."

"Ah a new question. It was Nastasiya. NKGB gave her Morse and secret code training. The Germans just teach their secret code. Was easy for them," the major smiled.

"So there was no handler for you here in Britain?"

"Nyet, nyet, nyet, no handler for us here, all by radio to France someplace, I don't know place, but not Berlin."

"Grischa, I am curious, what do you know about other Russian spies in England that are not part of your embassy, but are spying for Russia, not Germany?"

The major looked down at the floor for a moment, then looked up, stared past Tony and in a halting rhythm said, "I, don't control any. But, I know from a meeting, in Moscow, that they have, a source, in a high level office, like Parliament, MOD or Admiralty. I don't know more about that."

"What kind of information are they getting from this source," asked Tony.

"Don't know, don't know more. It was very secret thing. I grow sleepy now Tony. I am done now. Please."

Tony looked into Grischa's bloodshot eyes and nodded once sharply. Washington would be sure to pursue the questioning about the mole in London.

U.S. Naval Attaché Office
London

"How did it go with Kiminko?" asked Bill.

Tony shrugged his shoulders, "Best way to describe it is that he took a crushing blow. I left him in his quarters, told him to spend the rest of evening listening to music, having a good meal, drinking some gin and relaxing. He had already polished off the only bottle of vodka in the building. The doctor gave him something to calm him down and something to give him a good night's sleep before the debriefing continues tomorrow. I know Mike wanted at him before he got more rest, but I just decided to learn a few high interest items and let him be alone to grieve. In the current state he is in, knowing his personality, he'd be useless. I just finished giving Petra a rundown. I'll write up a summary of what I got out of him. By the way, two trinkets for you now, Nastasiya was the Doctor. Second, he said the Russians have a source in high British office, Parliament, MOD, Admiralty, he's not sure. And, he had no idea what kind of intel he's provided Moscow. He is apparently not in the loop for that one or is holding back, but I think he's just not involved with it."

Bill scratched his chin, "I'll be sure DC gets that item asap. I'll leave it up to Petra to take appropriate action. Write something up on that subject for me right away."

"OK boss, will do. I'm going to go talk to Mike when I leave your office. I have a few questions I'd like to have him ask."

"Oh, by the way. Lieutenant Jacob has worked out all the details with the Washington wheels. The Kiminkos will be taken to North Weald Airfield day after tomorrow to board an Army Air Force C-54 and fly to DC. Transportation from there, disposition of her remains and his interim quarters are almost completed. There are no problems, just paperwork and that will be wrapped up by the end of the day."

"Good. What a great time we had with all that, huh? I was going to spend the evening in Piccadilly tonight, then head back to Bletchley first thing in the morning, unless you have something else for me," said Tony.

"Bravo Zulu Tony. That's fine with me, but there's one more thing before you go. We have to go up and visit the Ambassador."

Ambassador Winant shook Tony's hand enthusiastically, "Commander, I've heard so many good things about you from Captain Taylor. It's a pleasure to meet you. Please have a seat." Captain Taylor nodded, smiling.

"Thank you, it's a pleasure to meet you Ambassador," said Tony as he took a seat next to Bill on the brown leather couch which sat on the window side of the Ambassador's office. Winant opened a right hand drawer, pulled out a manila folder and came around his desk to hand it to Tony "This is for you Commander. The Captain doesn't know about this yet, it just arrived in today's diplomatic pouch, but you may share it with him." Winant watched anxiously as Tony opened the folder.

Tony's face flushed, "Oh my God, I'm speechless." He stood and shook Winant's hand excitedly, "Thank you sir."

Bill stood and looked over Tony's shoulder. Inside the folder was a single sheet of White House stationery with a hand written note on it that said, "Tony, WELL DONE. I love a good cigar now and then." It was initialed in bold blue ink simply, FDR.

Wembley Park Flat
London

Tony and Petra were lying naked in the dark, buried under layers of blankets, wrapped up in each other's arms, basking in afterglow. The intensity of all they had been through in the prior week and the development of their feelings for each other culminated in a crescendo of emotions which they shared intimately. "I hate the thought of you getting orders one fine day. Bloody dreadful thought. I have wanted to end this a hundred times."

"I wouldn't have let you do that," he said. "Well, I would have railed against it, hoping to change your mind."

She giggled, "I can't believe I fell for a Yank. Especially when I know you're going to break my heart."

"Oh Petra, I absolutely won't do that. I have never ever seriously thought of getting married before, in fact, thought I could avoid it, but…,"

She interrupted, "Don't say it."

"Why?"

"Because," she paused. He waited. "Well, because," she whispered.

Tony laughed, "That's no reason."

She looked him squarely in the eye, "Let's be honest," she paused.

Tony felt his gut tighten, "I am guilty of having a roving eye when I first arrived. Searching I suppose, searching subconsciously. Finding thrill and fun, but never finding that soul mate. I didn't really think such a thing existed in other than the movies and novels. But slowly, I came to see that in you. The simple truth is, I finally found what I was looking for and I don't want to be with anyone else."

Her lips were quivering slightly and her eyes were teary. They embraced quietly for several minutes. They mulled over the many thoughts that were flowing through their minds. Had they come to a break point? Neither wanted that.

She kissed him softly, "Tony, you live in the United States, I live in Britain. When the war is over, we're both going to our homes thousands of miles apart. I have a child and, and, that's the bloody lot of it."

He smiled, wiped his eyes and hugged her tightly, "Petra, I can choose to leave the Navy after the war is over. I can choose to live wherever you'll be happy. I'll treat your son as though he is mine. I have the means and freedom to do all that easily. And that dear lady, is the bloody lot of it."

She thought intensely about what he just said, "I hope I don't regret it Tony, but I love you dearly." They embraced tightly in a long powerful kiss. "Let's see how this bloody war goes love. In the meantime, let's enjoy what we have."

Tony smiled and kissed her forehead, "Let's see what we can do to finish this damn war so we can get on with our lives, together."

* * *

GLOSSARY

Abwehr German military intelligence organization: espionage, human intelligence, Counterespionage, etc.

Admiralty British Royal Naval Headquarters

B-Dienst (German: Beobachtungs dienst) (English: observation service) A department of the German Navy Intelligence Service.

Bombe Electromechanical device created by British cryptologists for deciphering German military messages encrypted using an Enigma machine.

Bravo Zulu Also referred to as "BZ." This is a naval flag signal, typically conveyed by flaghoist aboard ship or other communications, meaning "Well Done"

By Your Leav In U.S. Navy parlance, a request for permission, usually in context with departure.

Callsign Sequence of alpha-numeric characters that identify the sending or receiving station in telecommunications of various methodology.

Cipher/Cypher Generally, a character for character encrypted plain text. Ci/Cy variants are U.S./U.K. differences in spelling.

Code Generally, a group of 1 to n alpha-numeric characters which has a specific plain text meaning each time it is used, e.g. A27 might mean, "commence firing" usually derived from a code book or other reference material.

COMINT Communications Intelligence; the exploitation of communications systems.

Crib   Cryptanalytic term for known or suspected plain text in an encrypted or encoded message that can be used to test for possible solutions.

DC-3   Douglas DC-3, a fixed-wing twin engine propeller-driven airliner.

Deep Draft   The **draft** (American) or **draught** (British) of a ship's hull is the vertical distance between the waterline and the bottom of the hull (keel), with the thickness of the hull included. Draft determines the minimum depth of water a ship or boat can safely navigate. Deep draft being characteristic of relatively large vessels.

D-Day   Military plans are developed often without the benefit of knowing the exact year(Y), month(M), day(D), hour(H), minute(M) or second(S) that the plan and its elements will be implemented. All elements of the plan's timeline are thus easily scaled from the establishment of the base moment. For example, an attack on an objective would be assigned the base timeline position of zero for YMDHMS. A preparatory activity scheduled 24 hours prior would be assigned, D-1. A post-attack activity planned one hour after attack commencement would be assigned the timeline position of D0, H+1.

DF   Direction finding/finder; measurement of a single line of magnetic bearing from a known location (DF site); intersection of lines of bearing from different DF sites determine the location of the signal transmitter.

DF Fix   Geographic location determined by multiple intersecting DF bearings.

DG   Director General (MI-5, but not limited thereto)

Enigma   Electromechanical rotor-based enciphering machine adapted and modified for military use by the Germans from a commercial version of the era.

FISH
Bletchley's codename for the decrypted product of the German Lorenz encrypted teletype communications system.

GC&CS
Government Code & Cypher School (aka Bletchley Park)

GRU
(Russian: *Glavnoye razvedyvatel'noye upravleniye*) Officially titled Main Intelligence Agency of the General Staff of the Armed Forces.

HFDF
High frequency (aka short-wave) direction finding/finder

HUMINT
Human Intelligence; information obtained from human sources (spy, interrogation, etc.).

Katakana
A Japanese syllabary, one component of the Japanese writing system along with hiragana, kanji, and in some cases the Latin script (known as romaji). The word *katakana* means "fragmentary kana", as the katakana characters are derived from components of more complex kanji. With one or two minor exceptions, each syllable (strictly mora) in the Japanese language is represented by one character, or *kana*, in each system.

Lorenz
German name for their high command encrypted teletype communications system used between Berlin and the German Generals and Admirals.

MI5
British domestic counter-intelligence agency

MI6
British agency that collects foreign intelligence aka SIS (Secret Intelligence Service)

MOD
Ministry of Defense, London

Modulated Continuous Wave (MCW)
A type of signal where instead of turning a carrier on and off, creating the dits and dahs of Morse code, a tone (such as one turned on/off by a More keyer) is mixed with the carrier (modulated).

NKGB
(Russian: *aródnyĭ omissariát osudárstvennoĭ*

ezopásnosti) Peoples Commissariat for State Security; conducted a wide range of intelligence and espionage activities, both offensive and counter.

OP-20G "Office of Chief of Naval Operations (OPNAV), 20th Division of the Office of Naval Communications, G Section/Communications Security", was the U.S. Navy's signals intelligence and cryptanalysis group during World War II. Located on the top floor of the Main Navy Building, Constitution Avenue, Washington, DC.

OpCen Admiralty Operations Center, London

Operation Chariot British commando raid on the Normandie dry dock at Saint-Nazaire, France conducted March 28, 1942.

Rezidentura Resident spy; Russian equivalent of a CIA Station Chief

Safford, Laurance Naval Officer that held various senior leadership positions in Navy COMINT efforts beginning in the 1920s, most notably while head of OP-20G prior to and during a good portion of WW2. He retired as a Captain in 1953.

Scuttlebutt A common Navy slang meaning rumor, gossip, idle chatter.

Shark The Bletchley Park code name for the German Navy's Triton encryption system.

SIS (see MI-6)

Station X Initially the overseas radio communications station at Bletchley Park, but later became the nickname for Bletchley in general.

Triton German Navy's code word for their 1942 reengineered version of the Enigma encryption system, that increased the number of encryption wheels from three to four making it (in their assessment) impossible to exploit due to the vastly increased encryption variables (see Shark).

ULTRA   A Top Secret (UK: Most Secret) information classification
             compartment originally created by the U.K. and
             subsequently shared with and adopted by the U.S. This
             was used to identify information gleaned from decrypted
             enemy communications considered operationally or
             strategically important. It was reported to a very restricted
             list of high level tactical, strategic or policy officials
             pertinent to the specific information.

VOQ   Visiting Officers Quarters

Wolfpack   German U-boat force tactic of operating a group of two or
             more submarines as a coordinated force to inflict more
             massive damage to assigned targets and to both confuse
             and disperse responding antisubmarine efforts.

Wren   Nickname for WRNS (Women in the Royal Navy Service).

Yeoman   An enlisted rating in the U.S. Navy with duties primarily in
             administrative and clerical work.

AUTHOR'S NOTE
Bletchley Park History

Documentation for the land that became Bletchley Park dates back to 1711. A land purchase filing in 1883 described the estate as having 581 acres. It remained so until May 1938, when Admiral Sir Hugh Sinclair, Royal Navy, head of the Secret Intelligence Service (SIS or MI6) bought 58 acres of the estate on which the manor home and primary buildings were located. Admiral Sinclair, obviously privy to high level intelligence on Hitler's activities, plans and policies, felt strongly that it was prudent to plan for relocating and expanding intelligence activities. Britain and France formed an alliance with Poland in an effort to deter Hitler from attacking any of them. Admiral Sinclair anticipated a probability of wider European hostilities, including Poland.. The potential of direct involvement by the United Kingdom in these hostilities heightened his sense of urgency. Admiral Sinclair found that there was no budget for facility acquisition to support the relocation and expansion of certain intelligence functions from London. Undeterred, the Admiral used £6,000 of his own funds to purchase the 58 acres. That specific location was selected due to its proximity to major road, rail, bus and perhaps most importantly, high capacity land-line communications resources. The initial contingent of MI6 staff relocated there from London on August 15, 1939.

Two days after Germany invaded Poland, Britain and France honored their alliance with Poland and declared war on Germany on December 3, 1939. The former manor home and country estate, Bletchley Park, was then fully funded and immediately began rapid development and expansion. Many MI6 functions that existed in London were moved to Bletchley. Recruiting of a wide variety of military, civil servants and civilian personnel ensued on an urgent basis. The "Mansion" soon became overpopulated while temporary buildings, which became known as "huts," were hastily constructed. Most of those huts still stand today. Construction subsequently began on concrete structures, named "blocks," were built to replace the huts and provide greater integrity against possible bombing. Expansion of functions resulted in the rapid growth of personnel to about 12,000 so the huts continued in use, some repurposed, until the end of the war.

After the Japanese attack on Pearl Harbor, full cooperation was established between the United States and the United Kingdom. in the conduct of COMINT operations and intelligence exchange.

The Bletchley Park story is very rich and interesting. Volumes have been written about it. Movies and TV series have been made of, or relating to it.

Readers can begin their journey into Bletchley's history and wartime operations by visiting the website managed by the Bletchley Park Trust: https://www.bletchleypark.org.uk/

ABOUT THE AUTHOR

Peter J. Azzole is a retired U.S. Navy Officer, a cryptology specialist, who served 20 years of active duty. The vast majority of his Navy career was spent in various facets of the field of communications intelligence. During his career, he served in several locations abroad, afloat and in the United States. His professional experience provides authenticity in the texture of this story.

This is Pete's second novel. His first, HELL TO PAY, is available via Amazon.com and other online bookstores. It is a historical novel about the early days of the Korean War. It is set initially in General MacArthur's Tokyo headquarters and aboard the U.S Navy aircraft carrier USS Valley Forge. The tale of the protagonist, a Navy pilot, involves air combat, romance, espionage, government corruption and much more.

Pete and his wife, Nancy, are enjoying their retirement in New Bern, NC.

Made in the USA
San Bernardino, CA
12 September 2018